For fourteen years no
been acknowledged to
top-selling science ficti
Originally published ir
Germany, the series ha
hardback and paperback in the States.

Over five hundred *Perry Rhodan* clubs exist on the Continent and *Perry Rhodan* fan conventions are held annually. The first *Perry Rhodan* film, 'SOS From Outer Space' has now been released in Europe.

The series has sold over 140 million copies in Europe alone.

Also available in the *Perry Rhodan* series

ENTERPRISE STARDUST
THE RADIANT DOME
GALACTIC ALARM
INVASION FROM SPACE
THE VEGA SECTOR
THE SECRET OF THE TIME VAULT
THE FORTRESS OF THE SIX MOONS
THE GALACTIC RIDDLE
QUEST THROUGH SPACE AND TIME
THE GHOSTS OF GOL
THE PLANET OF THE DYING SUN

Clark Darlton

PERRY RHODAN 12

The Rebels of Tuglan

Futura Publications Limited
An Orbit Book

An Orbit Book

First published in Great Britain in 1976
by Futura Publications Limited

This series was created by Karl-Herbert Scheer and Walter Ernsting, translated by Wendayne Ackermand and edited by Forrest J. Ackerman and Frederik Pohl.

ISBN 0 8600 7886 8

Printed in Great Britain by
Richard Clay (The Chaucer Press) Ltd.,
Bungay, Suffolk
Futura Publications Limited
110 Warner Road, London SE5

Contents

ONE

OF REBELS . . .

The alien was impish. The ludicrous little creature ducked into a depression in the ground and waited.

The world appeared to be dead. Flat sandy reddish hills stretched as far as the horizon, long valleys with sparse vegetation and occasional dried-out bushes. A dark red sun stood high in the sky, spreading a weird and literally *unearthly* light. It was cold, far below the freezing point. Here and there, vagrant stars twinkled forlornly in the very violet sky.

The only visible sign of life was the curious creature which looked like a considerably magnified mouse that was trying its best to become a beaver. Its tail was not long and pointed, in the typical fashion of normal mice, but broad and strong, like a beaver's, resembling the blade of a paddle.

The animal's body was about a yard in all, covered with a thick smooth fur that glistened reddish-brown in the rays of the dying sun. The pointed nose endowed the face with an expression of alertness and brightness.

Its very broad rump argued against its being a typically fleet-footed member of the rodent family. At least on dry land. It might be a quite different story in a river or lake. But unfortunately the lonely world of the dying sun had no water. At least not on its surface. And this was one of the reasons that the race of the mouse-beavers lived deep beneath the desert.

Life was monotonous and without hope but the mouse-beavers were satisfied with their lackluster lot. As long as the sparse vegetation supplied them with enough to eat, they knew no worries. As a *species* they knew no worries but there was this one exception among them, this being unique among its kind who, unlike the others, did not suffer a diminution of its intelligence when day was done. When the sun set, the wits of the others were extinguished like a candle wick. When night fell, their reasoning powers fell as well.

Not so, the little nameless one. It was but one of the huge colony living on this unknown and deserted planet, spending its days in grazing with the others who, after sunset, would crawl into their underground burrows to sleep. The sun would rise again in the morning and it would be time once more to feed; at nightfall, to sleep. Sun up, sun down, and life offered no diversions, no excitement.

Until the strangers came.

The astronauts from another world.

The spacemen from Earth.

They arrived in an inconceivably large sphere, descended from the skies and landed in the desert. They searched for something and after they found it they were ready to depart.

But they had brought something into this world for which the inhabitants had unconsciously been longing: variety and amusement. Especially strong was the compulsion to play in the heart of this one exceptional denizen of Vagabond.

Quivering with delight, the little mouse-beaver remembered the thrilling adventures and games it had experienced. The strangers – odd, upright-walking creatures with arms and legs – had brought along innumerable instruments and machines that made such wonderful toys. The strangers did not like at all when 'it' and the others would play with these machines; they had even been afraid. Why should they be afraid? Why were they so disturbed when the mouse-beavers had the heavy trucks run around in a circle and then started to activate all those interesting weapons? Wasn't that what they were intended for?

The mouse-beaver crouched lower down in the shallow depression. Not far from this spot, the giant sphere rested on the ground. The two-legged creatures were busily running back and forth, loading machines into the fathomless belly of their ship. Indeed, they wanted to leave this world for certain. But the mouse-beaver did not want them to depart. It would be so lonely and boring without these strangers. It was no fun just to play with boulders or sand. Of course, you could always make some friend rise up into the air and then let him drop to the ground again – but in the long run, even that became boring. What good was it to be able to move objects about without having to touch them, if there were no objects on this planet?

Now the strangers were finishing up with the work of closing some boxes. The mouse-beaver regarded the two-legged creatures, its head cocked to one side. It was wondering whether they would take it along if it asked them to. But – how should it ask them? They would not understand it. Maybe they were even afraid of it.

If it wanted to continue playing with these strangers, then it had to try to get inside the big ship. It had to join them and leave its own world. But how?

The boxes!

One of the boxes was quite close to where the mouse-beaver was hiding. The lid was lying next to the box, ready to be placed on top of it. The magnetic clamps would then automatically snap tight and close it. None of the two-legged creatures were in the immediate vicinity.

The mouse-beaver did not think twice. It acted instinctively and without too much conscious thought. It wanted to play, that was all. But this was only possible if it could get into the ship inside this box. The box, therefore, was its immediate goal.

It did not sit up on its hind legs the way its kind was wont to do, but crept instead on all fours, leaving the hollow dip in the ground. It used its broad tail to erase its track.

The animal – was it really an animal just because it did not look like a man? – reached the box, looked around cautiously in all directions and then disappeared as fast as lightning inside.

The mouse-beaver was lucky. It was one of the boxes used to store the food supplies for the space expedition. Part of the provisions had been used up meanwhile, and thus the animal found enough space to stow away its small body inside. The rest was easy.

True, one of the two-legged creatures who was standing at a distance, talking to one of his friends, was somewhat surprised to see the lid rise slowly off the ground, hover above the box and then slam down on top of it – but then he just shrugged his shoulders. By now the crew had gotten used to the more or less harmless telekinetic antics of the odd inhabitants of this planet. As long as they were satisfied to play with box lids, there was no need to sound the alarm.

And thus the mouse-beaver came into the big ship which two hours later left the home planet of the little creature, now flying toward unknown worlds it knew nothing about.

And the little mouse-beaver could not see how its home world, the sole planet of a dying sun, shrank gradually until it was a pinpoint of light, soon to vanish completely in the depths of the universe.

But it felt bored again!

It was dark and crowded in the box. The air was different. The oxygen-rich atmosphere aboard the ship was in crass contrast to the thin air of its home planet. Besides, it was terribly hot. The dying sun had supplied little warmth, and the temperature on the lonely planet the strangers had named Vagabond would sink way below the freezing point during the night.

The mouse-beaver started to perspire. It removed the lid and crept out of the box. At first, it was frightened by the room's size, but then it saw that there was box after box standing around. Must be a storage room.

Somewhere there were some noises. It lay flat on the floor and crept toward these noises. A door opened as easy as pie. Swiftly it slid through a long corridor. There was a hum coming from below. The metal floor was vibrating. There was another corridor on the right. The mouse-beaver turned into it. Then suddenly there was this smell.

Yes, a strange odor. It was warm.

All of a sudden a cold draft.

Another door. Two-legged creatures stood around talking in their strange idiom. Giant kettles were supported by pedestals. The two-legged ones were stirring something inside the kettles with glittering poles. The heat was unbearable.

The mouse-beaver caught a glimpse of a half-opened door. That's where the cold draft originated. The two-legged creatures paid no attention to the mouse-beaver. The big pots provided sufficient cover. A few leaps and it reached the door – and slipped through the narrow opening.

Soothing cold enveloped it. Strange smells were in the air. It let the door close behind it, and 'looked' around. It sent out waves like radar rays, which were reflected off the objects and produced an image on its sensitive retina as if by magic.

It felt hungry and it found a piece of fruit. The fruit was ice-cold and frozen solid, but it tasted delicious.

The mouse-beaver began to feel at home.

And then it started to play.

The system of the dying sun with the solitary planet fell away.

The gigantic spacesphere sped into interstellar space and prepared itself for the hyperjump through the fifth dimension.

The coordinates were fixed.

The sun Vega was exactly twenty-four hundred light-years away, nearly the same distance as Earth and its sun Sol. A distance beyond human comprehension but no problem for the spaceship *Stardust II*.

And definitely no problem for Perry Rhodan.

The commander of the giant craft, built centuries ago by the Arkonides, sat in his chair, ready for action. There was a steely glint in his gray-blue eyes. His slender tanned hands rested on the controls.

The small electronic brain had set the hyperjump coordinates. The scale showed 2401.073 light-years. The spaceship would dematerialize and, almost instantaneously reappear at the edge of the Vega system. From there it would not be too difficult to search out their destination by using the illuminated map they had found on the planet Vagabond.

Their destination – a lonely planet without a sun, forever wandering throughout infinity, toward eternity. It was the planet itself that harbored the secret of eternal life.

Rhodan waited a few more seconds.

He was filled with the restlessness of expectation. Too much time had passed already since they had set out on their search for the planet of eternal life. They had discovered its trace in the Vega system, followed it, but the unknown being had placed many obstacles in their way. He had laid down the trail of riddles to be solved throughout millennia, independent of time and space. But Rhodan and his friends had succeeded in solving all these tasks – except for the last one.

The Arkonide Khrest stood close behind Rhodan. His tall figure and long white hair gave him an awe-inspiring appearance. To judge by his exterior, it was hard to believe that his race was doomed, a victim of their own decadence. The Arkonides were the rulers of a mighty star realm, thirty-four thousand light-years distant from Earth. But this star realm was slowly and surely nearing its total collapse. Entire solar systems regained their independence and broke away from the commonwealth of the galactic empire. Khrest was one of the last survivors of the ruling Arkonide dynasty. He had set out on the search for immortality and was forced to crashland on Terra's moon. Perry Rhodan had rescued him while on his first manned lunar expedition and had brought him back to

Earth. Ever since that time, both he and Khrest were seeking the elixir of immortality.

They had come to the planet Vagabond, where they had found a further clue: a glowing map of the galaxy, showing a luminous trail leading from the sun Vega to the planet of eternal life.

With that they had finally conclusive proof of the planet's position.

Khrest sighed. 'Are you sure you want to start the transition now, Rhodan?'

'We have the correct coordinates, and not too much time, Khrest.'

The Arkonide shrugged his shoulders. 'We're still too close to the red sun; remember, this system has only one planet. It's easy to misjudge the distances under these circumstances.'

'Twenty astronomical units,' said Rhodan, glancing at the instrument panel. 'That's sufficient. Sit down, Khrest. We're ready.'

Khrest remained standing. It made no difference what the body's position was during a transition, since its own fields of gravity balanced out everything.

Perry Rhodan smiled with determination, then his fist hit down hard on the transition lever.

The stars disappeared from the videoscreen; all became dark.

All matter ceased to exist – at least in normal space – and slipped first into the fourth, then the fifth dimension, traversed a distance of 2401.073 light-years, independent of time and space, and finally began to exist anew.

2401 light-years?

The very moment the transition took place, Perry Rhodan realized that something must have gone wrong.

He felt the usual pain in his limbs, no different sensation than what he had experienced before. But his eyes could still see. And they perceived the figure on the dial of the coordinate scale race ahead madly.

Rhodan recognized a three, then another three, followed by three additional figures. Then he could not read the scale any longer; all grew hazy before his eyes, and turned dark.

Perry Rhodan and his spaceship raced, in a dematerialized state, through the universe toward an unknown destination.

The blue giant sun hung flaming and threatening in space.

This sun was the mother of thirty-eight planets, in various rotating orbital paths and receiving the sun's life-giving energy. Not all the planets enjoyed the sun's gift equally. The inner planets felt only its searing fiery breath. They were merely molten balls, held together by sheer gravity. Then came the zone of life. It extended from the eighth to the thirty-first planet. Beyond that giant ice worlds put an end to natural life. The outer planets were nothing but deadly ice-giants, lonesome and frozen solid, circling in ever-widening orbits around their distant sun which gave them only frugal light.

In the middle of the life zone, the planet Tuglan basked in the warming rays of its sun Laton. At night, Tuglan's sky was so full of stars that people could see their own shadows. No human being living on Earth had ever seen so many stars in the sky, for Laton was located at the edge of the star cluster M-13, in the Hercules constellation, more than thirty-five thousand light-years distant from Terra.

The planet Tuglan was inhabited.

The exploring space cruiser of the Arkonide star realm had discovered this fact more than six thousand years ago, and had quickly incorporated Tuglan into the galactic empire. For the Tuglanians this meant the beginning of an era bringing economic boom and technical progress. Space travel was developed, and soon after they were able to colonize the inhabitable planets of their own system.

Due to the contact with the Arkonides, political unification of Tuglan was achieved, and from that time on it was governed by the high commissioner of Arkon and the 'Lord of Tuglan.'

But the visits of the Arkonide spaceships to their distant colony came at greater and greater intervals, and contact between Tuglan and the faraway empire grew less and less. Only the presence of the high commissioner reminded the Tuglanians that they were the subjects of a far mightier power.

Properly speaking, however, the situation was still much more complicated. The Tuglanians were – although they no longer knew it – the descendants of the Arkonides. More than twelve thousand years ago, the first colonists had discovered and settled the planet Tuglan. At that time, the galactic empire did not yet exist as such in its later form, and therefore there was no longer any relation between Tuglan and Arkon. And, when the Arkonide explorers rediscovered Tuglan some six thousand years later, they believed they had found an entirely new race.

The Tuglanian descendants of the Arkonides had ceased to be albinoes, had violet hair now instead of the characteristic Arkonide white, and their complexion had become reddish-blue.

Hidden, feverish excitement reigned in the palace of the great Lord in the capital Tugla. Not a trace of this atmosphere reached the outside world, but the functionaries and dignitaries of the interplanetary realm of the Laton sun sensed that there was something in the air. However, they did not know what that might be, although many had some inkling.

The great Lord Alban, a tall man with hard features, made no bones about this as he talked to his younger brother Daros.

'It's been much too long that we have had to put up with the regimentation of these decadent Arkonides. Is there any valid reason why we should still be considered as one of their colonies?'

The younger man had far more pleasant facial features. His dark eyes revealed an expression of melancholy and softness but his energetic mouth bespoke a rather different disposition. He was slender and wore the regular clothing of a higher official.

He regarded his brother pensively. 'I realize that you would like to see the Tuglanians become an independent people. But let me answer you with another question: what advantage do you expect if we withdraw from the empire and become independent? Can you tell me any compelling reason for that?'

Alban impatiently waved aside his brother's objections with a gesture of his hand. 'What are the advantages of being a patriot, can you tell me that? Don't forget, the Arkonide empire is doomed. We don't hear too much, but just a few days ago the high commissioner let slip a remark which made it clear that the Arkonides have their difficulties. And many races think the way we do in this respect.'

'And what do we think, may I ask?' inquired Daros intently.

'We want to be free! Free from Arkon's rule! That's our slogan.'

'Free from Arkon's rule?' The younger man shook his head. 'That makes no sense. We have always been free men. I admit we're part of the Arkonide empire, but has this been to our disadvantage?'

'National ideals are at stake here!' shouted Alban with enthusiasm, hitting the table top with his fist. 'We have eight inhabited planets in our system and they're all united under my rule. We're strong and powerful. Why should we submit to the high commissioner's reign?'

Daros sighed. 'I don't follow your arguments any longer, brother. Why do you want to fight against someone who has done us no harm? The Arkonide commissioner is a peace-loving man. He doesn't interfere in our affairs. We're independent, if you look at it objectively.'

'Sure we are, but only because for a long time already we have rebelled against the Arkonide masters. It's just that we resorted to passive resistance, and not to force of arms. I regard the high commissioner simply as a relic from the past that must be removed.'

'You want to kill him?' said Daros, horrified.

'If necessary – yes. He controls the only radio communication we have with Arkon. If we interrupt it, he has no chance to warn the Arkonides. You see, I've thought of everything already.'

Daros cocked his head. 'You know that I don't share your ideas. Why do you confide your plans to me?'

The Lord of Tuglan smiled coldly. 'I have no son, brother, and someday you'll succeed me as a ruler. I want you to be a wise ruler. You should know the reasons for my actions in the future. In reality, you're to be envied. I shall free Tuglan; you, however, will be able to someday reign over a free race.'

Daros shook his head; he did not return his brother's smile. 'These are nothing but empty words, Alban. You can't free a people that is already enjoying freedom! Do you want to force us to become any happier than we are already? Don't we live in peace and prosperity? What improvements could your so-called freedom contribute to our present state of happiness?'

Alban's smile vanished. 'This freedom I want is a symbol, that's all. Nothing would be changed in our external situation, I agree. But just the feeling alone, not to have to obey anyone – well, just the very idea to be free . . .'

Daros rose to his feet. His dark eyes stared at his brother. A sharp line had appeared around the corners of his mouth. 'I don't share your opinions, Alban. You're the Lord, and the power over the realm of the eight planets rests in your hands. You must make the decisions. But I'm warning you: don't count on my support in this game. I would fight alongside you if I could see any sense in all of this. But this way – no, I'm sorry.'

Alban did not look at his younger brother. His eyes flamed angrily as he stared into a corner of the room. He spoke very softly. 'It might prove to be dangerous if you oppose me, brother.'

Daros smiled gently. 'Is that meant to be a threat? Who says I'm opposing you? I just don't agree with your plans, that's all. If you think I'd go to the high commissioner and betray your plans to him, you're mistaken. On the other hand, you're wrong to assume he won't find out about it. The Tuglanians are happy with their fate and aren't at all interested in becoming involved in a war that spells disaster.'

'We'll win this war.'

'What's the difference? Wars never bring luck to anyone, not even to the victors.'

'What nonsense!'

Daros impulsively stepped closer to his brother and grasped his hand. 'Alban, please be reasonable. Even if you should succeed in removing the Arkonide commissioner, you won't feel really free. Arkon's very far away from here, that's true. But one of these days Arkon will learn of our open rebellion. They'll send a punitive expedition – I prefer not to think what might happen to us in that case.'

Alban smiled again. 'There you are, Daros. Could we be called a free people if we're threatened with extinction? This threat hangs forever over our heads.'

Daros pulled his hand back. 'You don't understand me – or perhaps you don't want to understand me.'

Daros left the room, his head held high with pride.

Alban stared after him, a grim expression shrouding his eyes.

The high commissioner was a typical Arkonide.

To judge by his looks alone, one could have mistaken him for Khrest, but in reality he was even far more degenerate. He was incurably ill; he suffered from leukemia. Although a very intelligent person, he still was mentally and physically lazy. He did not take his duties any too seriously and limited his activities to occasional routine reports which he sent to Arkon. They always contained the same message: Everything is fine in the system of the Laton sun.

He almost never received a reply.

Even today's visit failed to rouse him from his usual lethargy. The young Tuglanian had asked to see him, claiming to bring an important message. The high commissioner received the visitor with a gread deal of reluctance.

'You're very late. I was just about to finish up here for today.'

The Tuglanian slumped into a seat. He looked utterly exhausted. 'You wanted to finish up for today? Unless you watch out, they'll soon finish you for good! Be careful!'

The Arkonide leaned forward in his chair. His searching eyes examined the visitor. The high forehead below the white hair was smooth and without a wrinkle. Commissioner Rathon was old and yet young-looking. And despite his mental sluggishness he was a very clever person. But he was also suffering from the hereditary defect of the Arkonides: He was overbearing.

'You're talking nonsense!' he interrupted the Tuglanian. 'Who would dare attack the high commissioner of the Galactic Empire? He would incur the wrath of a power that could destroy this solar system within a few seconds. Oh, why should I even get upset about such idiocies? My time's too precious, especially my leisure time. Good-bye!'

The Tuglanian remained seated. 'You think too highly of yourself and not enough of us. That's your national disease. If I'm willing to help you, it isn't because of your beautiful red eyes but only because of my love for my own people. I don't want war to break out between our two nations. Is that clear?'

'Why should it come to a war between us?'

'If you should be killed, then war will be inevitable,' the unknown visitor said brutally. 'And you can be sure you'll be murdered!'

Rathon began to feel uneasy. 'I'm the ambassador and special representative of the realm of the Arkonides, young man. Whoever attacks me, also attacks the Galactic Empire. Those who harbor such thoughts must also think at the same time of the destruction of Tuglan and its colonial planets. Who could be that stupid?'

'Someone is foolish enough!'

'Who?'

'The great Lord of Tuglan.'

It was very quiet in the room. Rathon sat motionless at his desk and kept staring at his visitor. Rathon was concentrating and thinking. The incredible news he had just heard seemed to have jarred him out of his habitual calm. But deep inside he resisted the notion that his tranquil existence might come to an end through such an extraordinary event. Life was too pleasant and enjoyable to have to undergo any changes.

'Well,' he said finally. 'The great Lord of Tuglan. Do you have any proof for your claim?'

The Tuglanian shook his head. 'There's never any proof positive for rumors, Rathon. I have a friend who works in Alban's palace and is the source of my information. It's rumored the Lord intends to disrupt any communication with Arkon.'

'Idle talk!' Rathon's voice was filled with scorn. 'I shall find out for myself that there's no truth and substance to this gossip. Tomorrow I'll go and see Lord Alban and ask him in person.'

The young Tuglanian leaped to his feet in alarm. 'No, Rathon! You can't do that! Not under any circumstances! Do you know what would happen to me and my friend if the Lord should learn of this betrayal?'

'If you've spoken the truth you'll be under my protection,' reassured the commissioner.

'Provided your protection will still be worth anything by that time,' muttered the visitor, and walked to the door. There he turned around once more. 'I implore you not to go to the Lord. Just wait and be on your guard, that's the best advice I can give you. Your life will be in great danger if you should alert Lord Alban.'

Commissioner Rathon waited until the door closed. Then he pressed a hidden button under the top of his desk. A videoscreen lit up on the opposite wall. The face of a man became visible. He was a Tuglanian, dark-haired and young. There was humble expectation in his eyes.

'Ror, come to my office. I have some work for you.'

TWO

... AND ROBOTS

Three robots tended the hyperwave broadcast station of the Arkonides on Tuglan.

The station was located in a geodesic dome on the outskirts of the capital. The building was surrounded by a high wall that provided more decoration than protection. For thousands of years it had never occurred to anybody to enter the area of the station.

A wireless energy line connected the broadcast station with the headquarters of the high commissioner. Rathon could obtain direct contact with Arkon, thousands of light-years away.

The three robots represented a top product of Arkonide electronics. They were equipped with mechanically working memory storage banks and were powered by a never-failing atomic battery. Their external appearance was that of a typical Arkonide, except for their metallic skin which gave away that they were nothing but machines.

They could execute all necessary manipulations with their right hand, to which they would attach any tools a particular job required.

Their left hand served exclusively as a weapon. The built-in pulse-ray gun was so powerful that it could destroy any enemy or attacker at a great distance. As long as these three robots had existed, they had never encountered any situation which would have necessitated the use of this weapon. The built-in locking device, which prevented any misuse by force, had never been broken so far. Their electronic brains had never had to draw the logical conclusion that these ultimate weapons ought to be used.

Until now the robots had been merely peaceful workers and silent guards.

Until this day.

The two shadowy figures stopped before the wall. The giant blue sun had long since set in the sky and the silvery starry night had replaced the dusk.

'That's the place,' whispered one of the Tuglanians almost inaudibly. 'Do you think the robots will give us any trouble?'

'Why should they?' whispered the other Tuglanian. 'They don't know what we plan to do. And besides, I don't believe they would attack Tuglanians. That's never happened before.'

'Nobody's ever come here intending to blow up the station,' replied the first man. 'But the great Lord is right: only if the communication with Arkon is cut can we obtain our freedom.'

'I don't understand too much about politics. I've always felt free and I can't imagine what greater freedom would be possible. But I'm sure the great Lord knows what he's doing.'

'Shh! I heard a noise behind the wall.'

Both men remained quiet, but they heard nothing more.

'The wall isn't too high. I checked it out yesterday and I found a good spot where we can climb over it. The rest shouldn't present much difficulty.'

They crept along the wall, the hand of the one Tuglanian searching along the masonry until he found some molding jutting out. He stopped suddenly.

'I've found it. I'll climb up first and then you follow me. Set the timer of the bomb for five minutes!'

'All set.'

'Okay. Watch it!'

The Tuglanian's shadow was sharply outlined against the star-studded sky as he sat astride the wall. He helped his companion up to the top of the wall. Then they waited and listened for any noises coming from the garden. Nothing stirred.

The roof of the cupola shimmered like silver in the light of the stars. At the highest point in the middle of the roof, they could see an antenna with a golden-colored sphere at its end, pointing into the nocturnal sky. That was all that was visible of the extensive installation.

'Where are we going to place the bomb?' whispered the Tuglanian who had been last to climb the wall. 'The roof's supposed to be made of an indestructible alloy.'

'Yes, it's made of Arkonite. We'll plant the bomb inside the station, of course.'

'Why so complicated? I'm convinced we could have vaporized the entire building with a halfway functioning ray cannon.'

'Oh, you fool!' exclaimed his companion furiously. 'It's supposed to look like an accident. Or maybe that the primitive inhabitants of Planet Thirteen carried out this attack. We mustn't be suspected at all.'

The first Tuglanian noticed some movement close to the geodesic dome. He ducked down and pulled the other down onto the top of the wall. 'Let's get down into the garden! The robots are on the alert. I don't know what will happen if they discover us inside their territory.'

They jumped off the wall. The soft ground muffled the impact. They crouched on the ground for a long time, watching the building. But there was no more movement there. All remained quiet.

Inside the dome, the three robots stood in front of the videoscreens. Impulse currents flowed through their brains and made contacts in the relays. Previously unneeded areas were activated. For the first time in thousands of years an alarm was given. The built-in loudspeaker came alive.

'Somebody has intruded in our garden,' Number Two stated calmly. Number One nodded his head, an almost humanlike reaction. The Arkonides had been clever and had purposely endowed their robots with emotions.

'Two Tuglanians, if the seeker speaks the truth. What do they want here? The thought-receiver gives no information.'

The third robot depressed several buttons, pulled some levers and stared at a small videoscreen which quickly filled with some abstract patterns. They whirled about in total chaos until they apparently presented an orderly picture. The robot absorbed the images and then said with his metallic voice:

'Their telepathic emanations are indistinct. As far as I can make out, they do not come as friends. Unfortunately their thought impulses are too weak. It will be difficult to find out what their plans are. But in any case they do not mean well.'

Robot Number One glanced at his left arm.

Number Two observed this glance and shook his head.

'There is no immediate danger, Number One. I will go out and ask the two Tuglanians what they want from us.'

'That would be wrong,' protested Number One. This was a demonstration of a new trend among Arkonide scientists. They constructed their robots not all according to one and the same scheme but gave them their own identities and individual thought processes. They had even identified them further by giving the robots numerical designations. Robots of the same type could therefore have different opinions. 'Go to the door and observe them, but do not let them see you. This way, perhaps, we have a better chance of finding out why they came here.'

RN2 disappeared.

On one of the screens the garden and its environs could be seen. The searching infrared rays conjured up a lifelike image on the ground glass screen. Even the faces of the two Tuglanians could be clearly distinguished.

They talked to each other and now one of them pointed toward the geodesic dome. Then both jumped down into the garden and hid behind some bushes.

'They have seen Number Two,' said RN3 calmly. 'Too bad.'

'Why is that too bad?' wondered RN1. 'On the contrary. They have given themselves away with this reaction. They do not intend to pay us a polite visit. That becomes evident from various factors. Firstly, they come at night and climb secretly over the wall. Their bad intentions are demonstrated, secondly, by the fact that they try to hide from Number Two. Now we know at least where we stand.'

'And what are we going to do?'

The eyes of RN1 seemed to glitter still more icily than

before. There was a cold fire in his crystal lenses.

'What does logic tell you?'

RN3 snapped back immediately: 'Defense!'

The two Tuglanians crouched waiting in the bushes for ten minutes. Then their patience came to an end.

'It was nothing,' whispered the politically inexperienced man to his comrade. 'We were mistaken.'

'I'm not so sure,' doubted the second man, but then he shook his head. 'Well, in any case, we can't afford to wait any longer. The robots cannot possibly know what we have in mind. Regardless whether they've spotted us or not, we must carry out the orders of the great Lord. I'll go first; you follow me. And have the bomb ready.'

The two conspirators reached the building. They still did not see any suspicious movements, for RN2 had long since returned inside the station and locked the door.

He reported: 'I am convinced they harbor no good intentions. We should ask them about it, Number One.'

'Maybe you are right,' the robot leader agreed. 'Unless we do something, they will remain outside and we will never learn what they wanted from us. Since nobody can penetrate the cupola, we have to open the door. So – go ahead!'

The two Tuglanians were still waiting. One of them fingered the time bomb nervously. He seemed not to know what to do with it. It was quite a shock when suddenly part of the curved wall slid aside. A robot stood in the opening.

The two Tuglanians were so scared to death that they could not move.

The robot addressed them in the Tuglanian language.

'Why have you come here? Do you not know that it is

forbidden to trespass on this station?'

The politically slightly more talented of the two conspirators regained his composure. He tried a friendly smile. 'We came to warn you,' he said. 'They're planning an attack on the radio station of the high commissioner.'

In vain, RN2 tried to probe the thought streams of the two Tuglanians, but they were too weak to release the necessary impulses.

'Who?' the robot asked distrustfully.

'A secret organization that rebels against the empire. The great Lord found out about it and asked us to warn you.'

'Why do you not go to Rathon? Why do you come to us, and in the middle of the night?'

'Nobody's supposed to find out about our visit.'

That sounded logical enough. RN2 pondered for a while. Behind him sounded the voice of RN1: 'What do they want?'

'They have come to warn us of a plot against us and the station!'

'Then bring them inside.'

The Tuglanian secretly pushed down on the button of the timing device.

The firing mechanism started up in the bomb he was carrying hidden inside his pocket.

Five minutes remained to deposit the bomb and then to escape to safety.

RN3 greeted his colleagues and the visitors with silence. The robot recognized a change in the colorful patterns on the thought-image videoscreen. This could lead to some interesting conclusions. He decided to be on his guard and to continue observing the Tuglanians.

In the meantime, the conspirator carrying the bomb in his pocket looked around feverishly for a place where he could deposit it. Five minutes could be a very long time – under certain circumstances. When you had to consider your own safety, however, five minutes were much too short.

RN2 walked behind his visitor, while RN1 led the way. He was filled with doubts. He did not know what to think of this visit. If it were true that the Lord of the Tuglanians had discovered the imminent attack on the Arkonide radio station, it would have been normal procedure to directly warn the high commissioner of Arkon. Instead, he sent two men to the station to warn the robots. That was not logical. There was something suspicious about the whole affair.

Could it be that the two men did not speak the truth?

That was easy to determine. RN1 made a sign to RN3. 'Watch the thought image screen,' he said. 'I will ask them something in their own language. Tell me if they are lying.' And he turned to the first Tuglanian: 'The Lord of Tuglan has sent you?'

The colored pattern of the abstract figures remained unchanged as the man hastily gave an affirmative answer. That was odd.

'And an attack on this station is being planned?'

'Yes,' was again the Tuglanian's reply.

Two minutes had passed.

On the thought image screen the figures began to intertwine and coalesce, finally assuming new shapes. The abstract configuration changed constantly. RN3 threw questioning glances in the direction of RN2 and nodded his head imperceptibly.

The two Tuglanians became very nervous. 'We came

to warn you. Be on the lookout. The conspirators will come tonight, we were told. We have to leave now.'

'Stop!' RN1 shook his head. 'Why such a hurry?'

The Tuglanian with the bomb looked around desperately. It was high time to depart if they did not want to go up in the air with the station. And the bomb was still in his pocket; he had not yet had a chance to plant it. Why should he risk his life?

He was standing next to a switch panel with a confusing array of levers and buttons. On a narrow bench beside it lay tools and spare parts. In between stood small boxes with screws, nuts and bolts needed for the repair of technical installations. Furtively, the Tuglanian pulled the small bomb out of his pocket and placed it among the boxes, where it would be quite inconspicuous.

RN3 observed a colorful whirl on the thought screen but he could not determine which of the two visitors caused it. He motioned to RN1.

Three minutes had gone by.

'We don't want to run into the conspirators here,' said the first Tuglanian. 'We've risked our lives by warning you. So let us go now.'

The patterns became quieter again. Indeed, they had risked their lives. Again no lie. RN1 could not make sense of this situation. Should he let the two leave? A feeling of uneasiness made him reluctant to let them leave.

The fourth minute came, and all of a sudden the tiny alarm bells of the hyperwave receiver began to light up. An Arkonide message sender announced himself. That was a most unusual and rare event, for the Arkonides maintained only very loose contact with Tuglan.

RN1 manipulated several levers with his right hand and concentrated his attention on a square screen next to the row of little lights. The loudspeaker below the row began to give off high buzzing sounds. On the screen appeared an image of the universe. In the midst of infinity floated a giant sphere like a planet.

'A battleship of the Arkonides!' muttered RN3. 'Distance – it is already inside the system of Laton. The ship's impending arrival was not announced at all via hyperwave radio signal. Why do they announce themselves so late?'

RN1 did not answer. He tried to regulate the volume control but could not establish a connection. And while he was still working at the controls the screen went dark and the loudspeaker grew silent.

The Arkonide sender had ceased to function.

There was no explanation for this.

Four minutes and thirty seconds.

The two Tuglanians suddenly whirled around and ran out of the room. They quickly reached the still open entrance door and made a dash for the bushes.

RN2 reacted instantaneously. His brain released the barring mechanism and changed his left arm into a ray gun. Awkwardly the robot set itself in motion and followed the fleeing men.

RN3 simultaneously arrived at the same conclusion that the two Tuglanians constituted a clear and present danger. Ten seconds later, the two robots searched the silvery darkness of the starry night with their crystal eye lenses and discovered the fugitives on top of the garden wall. A violet energy finger flashed and ended the lives of the two Tuglanians before they could jump to safety on the other side. The high Lord of Tuglan had lost two of his most faithful servants.

RN2 and RN3 turned around in order to return to

the geodesic dome. This was the instant when the five minutes had passed since the timer of the bomb had been activated.

RN1 had given up his attempts to reach the Arkonide vessel. There must be special reasons why the craft decided to interrupt its broadcast. Anyway, now it was the station's duty to inform the high commissioner of the latest happenings. The sudden appearance of an Arkonide spaceship must not necessarily mean good news. Inspections were never pleasant. In addition, there was the warning of an impending bombing attack. This was sufficient cause to awaken the commissioner in the middle of the night.

The moment RN1 established connection with Rathon's residence, the catastrophe happened.

The primitive bomb detonated to the right of RN1, hardly two yards away. The explosion ripped the thin Arkonite wall of the broadcast station and damaged the most delicate, irreplaceable parts of the actual transmitter. At the same time, the detonation started an accelerated energy conversion in the small reactor of the station's power plant, which in turn caused all the condensers and transistors to burn out as the current simply jumped across the burnt-out fuses.

A metal fragment hit the head of RN1. He lost consciousness in the true sense of the word, and stopped motionlessly in his tracks.

The next morning a conference took place behind locked doors between Lord Alban and the high commissioner Rathon.

The Arkonide looked haggard. No wonder, since he

and three robots faced an entire dominion with eight planets. And the news that RN3 had reported during the night was all but reassuring.

'This night a bombing attack was carried out against our hyperwave radio station. The installations were destroyed. Communication with Arkon has been disrupted. How can you explain all that?'

Rathon had uttered these sentences in clipped tones with an undercurrent of panic in his voice. Alban, the sly Lord of Tuglan, felt at once that Rathon had no idea who was behind this act of sabotage.

'I've already heard of it,' he said cautiously. 'Yesterday. I sent two men to warn you. It seems they came too late.'

'No, they went to the radio station and warned my robots. Five minutes after their arrival a bomb exploded. My robots mistook your messengers for the culprits and killed them. I'm very sorry. But their logisma-circuits had identified the men as enemies.'

'They're dead?' Alban said slowly. What a stroke of luck. More than he had hoped for. This meant that nobody knew that he had arranged for the destruction of the hyperwave transmitter. 'They were faithful servants of the galactic empire. They were only doing their duty.'

'One of the robots suffered damages, which can be repaired, though. The hyperwave station can never be used again. One of the generators is emitting harmful radiation which makes life impossible for any length of time within a radius of two hundred yards. Therefore, I've decided to transfer the robots to my own residence. I might need some personal protection in the near future.'

Alban did not respond to the account of Rathon's personal troubles. He was far more interested in something else.

'Communication with Arkon and the rest of the empire is cut, you say? Is there any possibility of informing Arkon of the incident?'

'Unfortunately no,' Rathon replied. 'Most regrettably. But I have another bit of news that will cheer you up, I hope. Shortly before the bomb went off and destroyed our installations, my robots received a radio signal on the hyperwave. An Arkonide battleship announced itself. Its picture even appeared on the videoscreen. Too bad the explosion occurred before proper contact could be established.'

'A battleship?' Alban shouted in fear. But he quickly collected his wits as he remembered that the hyperwaves had a practically unlimited range and need no time whatsoever to propagate throughout the cosmos. The battleship need not be in the vicinity of the Laton system; it might just as well be at the other end of the universe.

'Yes, it was just about to send us a message, when suddenly we were cut off. At the same time the bomb also exploded.'

'What a strange coincidence,' Lord Alban remarked thoughtfully. But his reprieve did not last long.

Commissioner Rathon continued: 'Our direction finder and range indicator showed that the battleship must already be within our system here. Actually I expect the spaceship to land on Tuglan at any moment now. We must prepare for this in any case. I wouldn't like to see you encounter any difficulties because of this bombing attack. Let's hope we'll find a plausible explanation for this incident. I'd like to suggest, however, that you proceed more energetically against the underground movement.'

'The Arkonide battleship – already here?'

Alban stared dumbfoundedly at the high commissioner. The whole world seemed to collapse around him.

THREE

THE 'IMPOSSIBLE' STOWAWAY

Perry Rhodan regained his sight; he saw an infinity filled with stars.

The leap through hyperspace had gone wrong!

Khrest approached. Silently he stared at the semicircle of videoscreens which rendered a lifelike picture of everything outside the ship. The closely placed screens created the illusion of a transparent wall. Nothing seemed to separate the two men in the Command Center from the emptiness of space.

Behind them a door slid aside. A stocky man with red, bristly hair entered the room, his pale-blue eyes staring in wonderment at the screens. He muttered skeptically:

'Somebody seems to have stuck the sky full of holes! Where do they come from?'

'That's a good question!' Rhodan countered sharply. He took his eyes off the starry sky image on the screens. Then he remembered something. Something that had happened during the transition. Hadn't he realized then that something had gone wrong?

Of course, the coordinates! The distance!

Now he saw the disastrous figures: 33,560.

Also the direction of the hyperjump was different than they had originally calculated.

Someone must have shifted the coordinates at the very moment of the transition.

The new arrival, none other than Reginald Bell, Rhodan's best friend and companion, seemed to intuit that something had apparently gone wrong. Khrest, his eyes half closed and his body rigid, was standing silently on the other side of the control panels. Rhodan's forehead was marked by a deep furrow between his eyebrows – always a sign that forebode no good. And besides – the final proof that all was not well – the sky was covered with entirely unknown constellations.

For an instant, Bell thought to recognize in this another fantastic mirage of the Great Unknown, whose trail they were pursuing; but he rejected this thought almost immediately. The immortal could not be so simpleminded as to pull the same trick twice. A being capable of manipulating space and time would never leave himself wide open like that.

Then must the unknown space out there be for real?

'Damn it, what's happened?' he grumbled, and stepped over to Rhodan. 'I'd appreciate some explanation!'

'Where are our telekineticists?' came Rhodan's counter question in place of an answer.

Although Khrest kept his eyes half closed, he was still listening in to the conversation. Bell's reaction to Rhodan's question was a feeling of irritation; he was not too pleased by his friend's apparent attempt to avoid the issue.

'What about our telekineticists? Do you want them to put the sky back in order, move the stars to where they belong?'

'Stop that nonsense now, Reg! I have a very good reason for wanting to know where they are. The controls were shifted right during the transition. Since only Khrest and I were in the Command Center during that time, it can only have happened by telekinesis. That's why I'm asking you where they are.'

There were three telekineticists in Rhodan's mutant corps – Betty Toufry, just nine years old; Anne Sloane, the young American girl; and Tama Yokida, the Japanese. Bell stared straight into his friend's eyes, just for a moment, before he turned on his heels without uttering a word. He left the room, finally convinced that the situation was too serious to permit any further fooling around.

Khrest moved. Rhodan had almost forgotten his presence. 'Do you really consider our mutants might have tampered with the coordinates, Perry?'

Rhodan shook his head. 'I hardly think so, but I wanted to make absolutely sure. No, they wouldn't be that foolhardy and risk their lives. If we weren't so far away already from the planet Vagabond, I'd be inclined to believe that those crazy mouse-beavers had played another of their tricks. But it's most unlikely; the distance is too great.'

Bell returned a couple of minutes later, his big round eyes filled with misgivings. 'The mutants had definitely nothing to do with this calamity. Who else could it be? The mouse-beavers, maybe? But we were already too far away. Where are we now?'

Rhodan did not know which question to answer first. Neither could he decide which for the time being was more important. Khrest solved the problem in his own way.

'If I'm not mistaken, I know this sun over there,' he said, pointing to a giant blue star positioned at an angle to their flight direction. The star's light was so bright that Rhodan had to shield his eyes. 'I shall check up on it in the map room to make sure I'm right in my assumption.

But I think it would be wise to double-check, Perry. Would you please, meanwhile, find the exact angle of deviation from our intended course? Also the distance we've jumped across.'

Khrest left the room without waiting for a reply.

'How could that have happened?' groaned Bell. 'To miss our destination so badly!'

'We were exactly two-thousand light-years distant from Vega when we started the transition. However we jumped not two thousand four hundred but over thirty thousand light-years. In addition to that, we changed our direction – as far as I've been able to determine – by about sixty degrees. This means we're now thirty-six thousand light-years removed from Vega. What a mess!'

'You said it,' grumbled Bell, beside himself with aggravation. 'And you're quite sure the navigational brain made no mistake?'

'Absolutely!'

'I can't make any sense of this whole situation!'

They fell silent for a while until Khrest returned to the Control Center. In his hand he held a small replica of a map, a paper-thin plastic card with innumerable dots and crosshatched lines.

'I've had them make a copy of this map, Rhodan. Look here!'

He pointed to a pale giant star. 'That's Laton, a huge sun with thirty-eight planets. It's registered in our index here on the *Stardust*; it's a part of our empire. We were lucky after all. We should be able to obtain the necessary data there for the transition to Vega.'

Rhodan did not seem especially thrilled. 'Do you think we'll encounter any Arkonides on this planet?'

'At least one administrator, the high commissioner

from Arkon. Our colonial races have kept their independence, and we leave in their hands how they wish to govern their own systems. According to the index, Laton has eight inhabited planets. One of which is called Tuglan, the eleventh planet, the main seat of our administration. We can land there without any fear.'

Rhodan noticed the secret joy Khrest experienced. It had been over four years that the Arkonide scientist had been cut off from any contact with his home planet Arkon. Ever since he had to crash land on Earth's moon, where he had been rescued by Rhodan. So far Rhodan had cleverly prevented Khrest from re-establishing communication with Arkon. He did not want the mighty lords of the empire to learn of Earth's existence, for fear they would incorporate it into their realm.

Not until Terra was sufficiently strong and united would it be advisable to take up contact with Arkon.

On the other hand, if Rhodan were to refuse now to land on one of Arkon's colonies, he would certainly incur Khrest's displeasure. Quite apart from Thora's reaction.

Thora, the female commander of that Arkonide space cruiser on which Khrest had held the position of leading scientist, hated Rhodan because he was a human being. And she loved him because he was a man. But she longed with all her heart for her home planet, Arkon. She would cause a great deal of trouble if he were to refuse landing on Tuglan.

Rhodan quickly arrived at a decision: 'We'll establish contact with Laton, Khrest, under one condition – don't reveal the location of Earth to your commissioner there. I don't believe this is the right moment for it. You know the reason why, no doubt.'

'I do,' Khrest reassured him. 'And you know that I share your feelings in this respect. During the past four years I had ample opportunity to get acquainted with the human race and to appreciate their special talents. We're agreed, Perry, that Arkon's might is nearing its end. If there should ever be any successor to our galactic empire, it could be only the human race, the Terrans. But what about Thora? Will she also agree?'

Rhodan could not answer that question for an alarm bell began to ring loudly.

Rhodan rushed over to the ship's intercom at the back wall and found out that the alarm originated from the galley. For a moment Rhodan was confused, for nothing was more improbable now than that something unusual should have happened there of all places.

He depressed a lever. A tiny videoscreen lit up. The face of an agitated chef filled the screen.

'Commander Rhodan!' he burst out before Rhodan could ask him a question. 'We have a stowaway on board! Could you come to the galley at once, sir?'

Rhodan was thunderstruck. He could not even inquire who the stowaway might be. By the time he caught hold of himself, the cook's face had already disappeared from the darkened screen.

'A stowaway?' asked Khrest. 'Who could that be?'

Rhodan shut his eyes for an instant. Then he said: 'I'm going to the galley. Why don't you come with me, Khrest and Reg?'

The three men left the Command Center. On the way, Bell was busy with his thoughts.

A stowaway? Nobody could have gotten on their spacecraft in the middle of deep space. And there were no human beings, besides the ship's crew, on the planet

Vagabond, the last place they had touched down.

Bell had arrived at this point in his deliberation when he was struck by a sudden insight. His mouth became a thin line, his eyes narrowed to a slit.

'Of course!' he yelled as the three were about to jump onto the first antigrav lift, which then plunged them rapidly down into the depths of the space vessel. 'A mouse-beaver! I should have known it at once.'

They stepped off the antigrav lift and onto a moving walkway. The kitchen came into sight. They were still quite far away when they became aware of something unusual going on there. Men were running about, all excited; the cooks were swinging their big spoons like a club, trying to drive the radio personnel and the technicians from their domain.

Rhodan and Bell pushed their way through the crowd and entered the kitchen. The big glittering kettles were deserted; no one seemed to bother about getting the next meal ready. Instead, an excited group of men had gathered at the other end of the big galley, talking, laughing, gesticulating wildly. Indescribable chaos reigned, but nothing indicated that there was an immediate threat to anyone's safety.

The head cook discovered Rhodan and hurried toward him. 'That damn beast!' he shouted. 'It must have slipped on board while we were loading on the boxes with our provisions. If I get my hands on the guy who's responsible for this, I'll ...' He accompanied his words by whirling a huge soup ladle over his head.

Rhodan raised his hand. 'Quiet! Shut up! Have you all flipped your lids?'

'That damned mouse-beaver!' gasped the breathless head cook, who had finally reached Rhodan. 'It sneaked in, and look at it! Gobbling down our food!'

The heavy-set cook pushed the onlookers aside, using his fat belly cleverly to butt the people out of the way, so that Rhodan and his friends could pass through a narrow gangway. They came to a heavy door with a sign, *Freezer Locker*, where the crowd was thickest. The door was open.

The mouse-beaver sat on its fat behind amidst a pile of frozen fruit. It held something skillfully in its front paws and nibbled at it with obvious delight. From time to time it would look up, blink at the onlookers as if to say: Tastes mighty fine, folks – much obliged for the treat!

Rhodan regarded the scene, undecided what to do about it.

There was no doubt in his mind that the mouse-beaver must have shifted the controls just before the *Stardust* had gone into transition. The little fellow simply had obeyed an uncontrollable impulse of its playful nature when it had messed around indiscriminately with the coordinates. Its telekinetic abilities were quite sufficient for that. Its action had thus endangered the lives of all aboard and must be punished. Furthermore, it was a stowaway. And in such case the laws of space travel provide extreme punishment; ejection from the ship without a spacesuit!

On the other hand, the mouse-beaver had not acted with evil intentions. It was a basic fault of its race to indulge in play at any time and anywhere.

But the law demanded punishment for the wrongdoer. Even one as charming as the furry little rodent.

Bell stood next to Rhodan and stared at the strange creature which displayed no signs of fear. It did not suffer from a bad conscience and probably had an idea that its droll appearance added considerably in improving the mood of these two-legged beings.

The mouse-beaver grinned and showed its single large incisor tooth. It was such a funny sight that several of the amazed men burst out laughing. Only Bell did not feel like laughing. This beast had caused them no end of trouble and had endangered all their lives by displacing the *Stardust* from its proper course. Now they were in some unknown part of the universe. Not even the mouse-beaver's cute looks could alter anything there.

Before Rhodan could intervene, Bell rushed toward the jolly rodent and grabbed it by the scruff of its neck. He jerked it upward with one violent move, screaming at it: 'You filthy beast! Not enough that you steered our ship into some sticky part of the Milky Way – you have the gall to stuff your face with our strawberries! That's the limit! We'll kick you out of here and let you float through the vacuum outside! But first you'll get a taste not only of our food, but of a sound licking!'

And before anyone could prevent it he soundly smacked the screeching little fellow's broad backside with his hand.

In the same instant, something strange took place.

The mouse-beaver wrangled itself free from Bell's grip and dropped to the floor. With one mighty leap it dived into the freezer locker and took cover. There it squatted on its sore bottom, eyeing Bell all the while with close scrutiny – and this is when Bell started to float in the air.

He seemed to have lost all weight, and drifted off like a balloon, past the dumbfounded head cook, in the direction of the big pots on the stove.

In vain did Bell try to kick his legs in order to change

his direction. His hands groped wildly around but nothing was near enough that he could have held onto it. The powerful telekinetic currents, generated in the mouse-beaver's brain, kept pushing Bell on and on.

The head cook almost had heart failure when Bell stopped just above the soup kettle. The thick broth simmered gently, dangerously close to Bell's bottom. Another inch and he would get badly burned!

But fortunately Bell kept drifting on toward another big pot. Despite Bell's valiant, desperate efforts, violent thrashing of his arms, he sank lower and lower into the big kettle. As luck had it, the pot was filled with water – cold water. There the man sat in the pot, his head peering pitifully above the rim. Rhodan, who had followed the incident with secret pleasure, started to laugh out loud.

The rest of the men followed suit, and the poor fellow, looking much like a missionary in a natives' stew pot, was quickly surrounded by the entire kitchen personnel and the crew.

'What a place to take a bath, Reggie!' shouted someone disrespectfully from the background. Rhodan came over and rescued his friend from his predicament. Dripping and shaking like a wet pup, Bell stood shivering beside the cooking pot.

Meanwhile, the mouse-beaver sat undisturbed amidst the frozen fruit piles, munching away at its heart's content. After all, who could be sure how long these two-legged creatures would tolerate its presence here?

'You'd best go to your cabin, Reg,' said Rhodan. 'And if you should meet John Marshall on your way there, send him here. And in the future I would recommend you not to wallop our stowaway. As you see, it's defending itself quite effectively.'

'Do you intend letting it stay on the *Stardust*?' snarled Bell, but he knew at once that even he would be unable to do away with the little fellow in cold blood. 'If it keeps on playing tricks like that...'

'This is why I want to see Marshall. Perhaps he can manage to establish communication with the mouse-beaver. Just tell him to come here, will you?'

Bell started to move and left a long wet trail behind. Rhodan returned to the freezer locker.

The mouse-beaver looked at him with large, expectant eyes. In its delicate hands it held a piece of fruit which it was nibbling, somewhat embarrassedly, it seemed. Its big round ears vibrated gently.

It looks at me like a dog, thought Rhodan, and felt a wave of sudden compassion well up in him. This creature was the product of another, strange planet. It did not originate on Earth. It was alien, it was otherworldly. Yet, he liked it.

It was an inexplicable feeling of sympathy, based solely on the droll appearance of the uninvited guest. Who could say, maybe the big, pleading eyes had a part in it. They seemed to say: please, don't harm me!

Against his will, Rhodan had to smile at the little fellow. The mouse-beaver returned the smile, grinned and bared his one and only tooth. At that moment the creature ceased to be an 'it' and became a 'he.' Rhodan knew they had become friends, but little did he realize that his friendship would turn out to be very close and lasting. For the mouse-beaver was not only a telekineticist – but that's another story.

John Marshall, the first telepath of the mutant corps, came into the galley. Bell had prepared him for what to expect. Therefore he was not especially surprised to find the mouse-beaver in the kitchen. He suppressed a smile as he asked Rhodan: 'So that's the little guy who helped Bell to an extra bath today?'

'If I'm not mistaken, Bell won't hear the end of that story for many years to come,' replied Rhodan with a chuckle, then pointed to the munching guest in the freezer locker. 'Try to establish contact with him. Perhaps you can read his thoughts – if any. More important still – try to communicate our thoughts to him. Will that be possible?'

John Marshall nodded his head in assent. 'Absolutely! Of course, all will depend on how his brain will react. Any indications as to his intelligence?'

'I should think so. He has mastered telekinesis, a pure mental force. We can presume, therefore, that his brain is well developed, especially well. Go ahead and try!'

Hardly a few seconds had passed when Marshall was seized by an extraordinary excitement. He nodded his head several times and spoke to the mouse-beaver, who listened attentively. Then the grinning tooth showed again in the wide-awake face. The creature squeaked a few times, quite amused, before replacing the partially eaten fruit in a box. He raised himself up on his hindlegs and walked solemnly from the freezer room toward Perry Rhodan.

'He wants to greet you,' said Marshall. 'He has had no trouble understanding me. His thoughts are easy to read and he can read ours if he activates a part of his brain that has gone unused till now. He has the makings of an excellent esper.'

Rhodan bent down to shake hands with the mouse-beaver. 'We'll call you ... Emby ... for the time being,' he said cordially. And he carefully took hold of the creature's delicate little hands. 'If you understand what I'm saying, just nod your head.'

'Emby' indicated his comprehension at once.

'So you can understand my words; that's fine! Too bad it's not so easy the other way around, since I'm not a telepath. But you'll learn our language. This man here will help you with it.' And he pointed to Marshall.

Once again Emby nodded his head and uttered a few shrill cries, obviously to express his delight. He whirled around and around and suddenly started to walk up the wall and onto the ceiling. There he performed an aerial somersault and returned to the ground.

'Very nice,' praised Rhodan, but raised a warning forefinger. 'However, in the future you must not play unless I give you permission to. Come along with me, I'd like to explain to you the mischief and trouble you've caused us. Afterward you can return here and eat as much as you want.'

The *Stardust* raced into the system of the Laton sun at the simple speed of light, crossing first the orbit of the outermost planet. The thirty-eighth planet, a gigantic ice world, passed by leisurely. Then the thirty-seventh planet, also uninhabited. The spaceship kept thrusting toward Tuglan, a world belonging to the great star realm of the Arkonides.

Rhodan, Khrest, Thora, Bell and John Marshall were gathered in the Command Center. Emby sat obediently in a corner of the room, trying to sort out the many thought streams that impinged upon him. He realized that his playfulness had caused a most unpleasant situation for his two-legged friends. They had forbidden any further fun games. Later on, after they would land somewhere, he would be permitted to play at his heart's content.

He would make sure to remember that promise.

'You're afraid, aren't you?' Thora asked sharply. Her eyes flashed a challenge at Rhodan. Bell, who had changed into a dry, freshly-pressed uniform, mumbled something incomprehensible, but otherwise refrained from speaking. 'Do you really believe I'm not aware how reluctantly you respond to our proposals? You're afraid the commissioner on Tuglan might send a report to Arkon – and that would mean the end of your eternal hide-and-seek game.'

They're talking about games, thought Emby.

'Nonsense!' countered Rhodan and cast an imploring glance in Khrest's direction. 'Why don't you, for once, try to understand my position? And if you can't do that, then remember our agreement: first of all we shall find the planet of eternal life, then we'll fly to Arkon. But not one minute sooner! Khrest is willing to abide by this agreement – I expect the same from you.'

'What has all of that to do with Tuglan?'

'Quite simple: I don't want the Arkonide high commissioner to find out anything about Terra. No more and no less. Therefore I must have your word of honor that you won't give him any information about us and Earth. We'll pretend to be the inhabitants of some colony of the galactic empire. We'll play a harmless game of deception.'

Emby pricked up his round ears. Here they went again, these two-legged creatures, talking about *playing* and *games*. Were they also as fond of games as he himself? They seemed to grow more likeable by the minute. Too bad they had forbidden him to play!

Why not try it again?

Over there, those sparkling instruments!

Rhodan spun around so fast that he almost knocked Bell over and into the wall next to him. The hyperwave transmitter started up on its own. Lights lit up, small videoscreens began to glow. The impulsators generated meaningless signals, fed them into the central station where they were transformed and beamed out into space.

With one mighty leap Rhodan reached the switchboard and slammed down a lever. The broadcast was interrupted immediately but it must nevertheless have been received somewhere already for the receiver continued working independently a while longer. It fed a code signal into the loudspeaker. On one of the vids appeared the picture of the metallic face typical of an Arkonide robot. Suddenly the image vanished as Rhodan depressed another lever into the off-position.

Rhodan swung around swiftly and walked slowly toward Emby.

The mouse-beaver cowered in fright and began chirping in his incomprehensive language. His big, round eyes looked imploringly at Rhodan, with the mute promise to be truly obedient from now on. A large tear rolled down the little fellow's hairy cheek.

Bell pushed his chin out aggressively and shook his fist threateningly at the playful wrongdoer.

Rhodan came to a halt in front of Emby. 'Marshall, I'd like to know why he did that just now! He understands me, but I can't make out what he's saying. What does he have to offer in his defense?'

The telepath bent down to the little fellow and peered into his round, sad eyes.

'Well?' he urged the mouse-beaver. A few seconds

later he straightened up. 'He promises never to repeat this game. He says we were talking all the time about playing, so he thought it would be all right for him to start up again with his favorite occupation.'

Rhodan turned to the stowaway from Vagabond. 'If you ever move any object here without my permission, I'll have you thrown out of this ship! Got that? Do you realize what you did? You've drawn the attention of some unknown race onto us and they aren't as friendly as we are. Quite possibly they'll kill you if we meet up with them. Just watch out from now on! Behave yourself and stay in your corner! Bell, keep an eye on him!'

'Why me of all people?'

'You must make friends with Emby. The sooner you get used to him – or vice versa – the better for all of us. I think this fellow will become a valuable member of our mutant corps.'

'The mutant corps?' gasped Bell. 'This maverick Mickey Mouse is supposed to become a part of our crack corps? That's too much for me . . .'

He broke off his protest as his feet left the ground, hovering a few inches above the floor. Just a few seconds, then he touched down again very gently. Emby wanted to give him a gentle reminder. Bell fought against his pride, then said: 'Okay, then . . . for all I care. He might be useful if he behaves. Is that a deal, Emby?'

The mouse-beaver nodded his head very seriously.

Rhodan stifled a grin and turned to Khrest. 'Our situation is changed now, since someone has noticed our presence here. The intensity of their signal leads me to assume that it came from a station inside this system.'

Khrest observed: 'I can't see that this should change anything but the only thing I'm worried about is how to explain your presence to them. The Arkonide commissioners have detailed lists of all our colonies – and your race isn't contained in them.'

Bell turned around. 'Then we'll simply change ourselves into Arkonides.'

Rhodan did not reply. He just stared at Bell. Khrest spoke up. 'Not a bad idea. It can't do any harm – besides, it'll be fun. But how can we go about it?'

'We have our medics aboard, they can help us. They can fit us with red contact lenses so that our eyes will look like those of albinoes. It will be easy to dye our hair white. That's all we need.'

'Dye our hair white?' stammered Bell.

'It will be only temporary,' Khrest reassured him. 'Also, there's another reason which makes this masquerade advisable. I had the opportunity to read up on the Laton system in our ship's library. The natives, the Tuglanians, have always offered passive resistance. I'd suggest, therefore, that we pretend to come there as a review board. Our representative in Tuglan will certainly go along with us; it's in his own best interest.'

Rhodan frowned. 'You lose sight of our original destination and purpose for this trip, to find the planet of eternal life, Khrest.'

Khrest smiled indulgently. 'This interlude might prove very advantageous for you and Terra, Rhodan. Show us how colonial races should be dealt with! Demonstrate that you can handle even totally unexpected situations, for we certainly have no idea what will await us on Tuglan. However, if the station that answered our broadcast signal should really turn out to be our hyperwave station on Tuglan – everything should be in the best of order there. Nevertheless...'

Rhodan understood what Khrest wanted. Perhaps he was right with his suggestion. He nodded his consent.

'All right, Khrest. Bell, inform Doctor Manoli to get his makeup kit ready for us! I'm willing to put on a terrific act!'

FOUR

TREACHERY ON TUGLAN

It did not make sense to Alban.

'How could they have heard about it so quickly!' he kept repeating to his younger brother. 'The battleship must have come the same instant the Arkonide radio station blew up. Do you have any idea who's behind this bombing attack, Daros?'

Daros looked long at his brother. Then he shook his head. 'Why do you try to deceive me, Alban? Didn't you yourself tell me about your plans? It was your own agents who destroyed the station; now you must bear the consequences for what you've done. I can't help you.'

'We're all in the same mess now, regardless of whether we're for or against the Arkonides – they certainly won't make any distinction here. The high commissioner must have warned his home base on Arkon before the attack took place. I didn't think he had that much intelligence. The Arkonide rulers are very powerful for sure, but they're also decadent and undecided. If it weren't for their super weapons we could easily finish them off.'

'One shouldn't underestimate one's opponent, for that's always the first lost battle,' warned Daros. 'But I have to disappoint you, brother. I'm not willing to risk my hide for you. I was and I still am against any rebellion.'

Alban placed both hands on the table in front of him. He fixed his younger brother with a stare. 'This makes us enemies, Daros. I fully intend to deceive the Arkonides. If the commissioner really gave the alarm, then the Arkonides won't find any cause to lead them to suspect *me*. The two men who threw the bomb last night are dead. Nobody knows on whose behalf they were acting. I shall, however, order my police to arrest several members of the revolutionary movement and have them executed as soon as the Arkonide punitive expedition arrives. This should clearly demonstrate my loyalty to their cause.'

Daros regarded his brother, and he was filled with loathing. 'You plan killing your most faithful followers, just to put yourself in a favorable light? That's horrible!'

Alban smiled slyly. 'You ought to be grateful to me.'

'Grateful? What for?'

The high Lord of Tuglan continued smiling. 'Because I won't tell anyone that you gave the order to the two criminals to blow up the broadcast station. You wanted to eliminate the Arkonides in order to usurp the position of high Lord of Tuglan in my place, after having gotten me out of the way, too. That's what you planned, brother, didn't you?'

Daros was speechless. How inconceivably low and treacherous his own brother had become! To turn the tables on him and blame him for everything! The Arkonide inspectors would believe him and fly home reassured that all was well on Tuglan. They might even insist on punishing the guilty traitors and then Alban could execute his younger brother, whom he believed to be a rival and who was much more popular with the people.

Daros began to realize the danger that threatened him. True, he had no proof whatsoever *against* his older brother. Their conversation of the previous day had taken place under strictest privacy. There were no witnesses.

'The Arkonides are too smart – they'll see through you, Alban. They're well acquainted with the psychology of their colonial nations . . .'

'I've thought of that, too, Daros. I've already arranged that some of our rebels will be apprehended during the visit of those albinoes. They'll all confess as one man that they want Tuglan to become independent and plan to get rid of their present Lord because of his loyalty to the galactic empire. Their new Lord, they will say, is called Daros. He desires freedom for Tuglan and the realm of the eight planets.'

Daros was seized by sudden panic. 'You'll find no one willing to sacrifice his own life for a lie.'

'Who says they're lying?' asked Alban, raising his eyebrows. 'They'll be convinced they're speaking the truth. Not even a lie detector could expose them as liars. No, dear brother, I've thought of everything. Others will state that they were incited to murder Rathon by your delegates, but that they refused to do so out of loyalty to the Arkonide empire.'

Daros clenched his fists. 'I really ought to kill you . . .'

'Just try!' Alban grinned perfidiously. 'That, too, I've taken into consideration. Look at my hands! They're resting on this table top, but also right on a button. A slight pressure will be enough to erect an instantaneous energy wall between us. You can't get to me – not even with force.'

'You devil!'

'Only the devil will be the final victor, all the others are too weak. Freedom-loving spirits need too much time to make a decision, because they always have to consider the welfare of their nations. I don't have to be bothered with such considerations; I can act at once. I don't have to ask anybody. From one second to the next I can make up my mind what to do; the opponent hasn't a chance to adjust to it, there's simply no time. Do you understand now why I shall be the victor and you the defeated?'

Daros forced himself to remain calm. 'I'm surprised you give me warning. Can I leave the palace if I want to? Am I free?'

'Of course my dear brother. The farther you flee the more the Arkonides will be interested to catch you. They'll interpret your flight as a confession of your guilt. Is that clear?'

It was all clear. Daros was caught in a trap. If he escaped, he declared himself guilty. If he remained in Tuglan, Alban's 'proofs' would finish him off.

'All right then, I shall stay. I have trust in the cleverness of the Arkonides.'

'And I rely on their stupidity. We'll see who's right. Now leave me, I'm busy. I have my hands full, preparing everything for a fitting reception of the Arkonide punitive expedition. I have to convince them of my devotion. My first word to them will be a complaint against the rebels.'

Daros got to his feet and walked to the door. He opened it and then turned around once more.

'When did the Arkonides visit our system last?'

Alban looked up unwillingly. 'Almost fifty years ago. When they brought the new commissioner here to relieve his predecessor.'

'A lot can change in fifty years.'

A lot would depend on the wisdom and cleverness of the Arkonides, thought Daros.

As they swung into orbit around the thirteenth planet,

Rhodan located three heavy space-cruisers drifting along slowly. They were armored and therefore recognizable as warships. Khrest ordered the normal radio transmitter to be used.

'Will we be able to understand them?' asked Rhodan.

'They speak Pankosmo, the Esperanto of our empire. And you, Rhodan, have learned this multiplanetary language together with Bell, Haggard and Manoli during your hypno-training four years ago. It won't present any difficulties for you, therefore, to understand the Tuglanians and make yourself understood by them. This very moment John Marshall is undergoing a hypo-indoctrination of Pankosmo. It will be to our advantage if one of our telepaths can communicate with the Tuglanians, too.'

A signal from the radio station told that contact with the three spaceships had been established. Rhodan switched on the videoscreen and looked at it with great interest. At first he saw the three ships; then the face of a man appeared.

Alban, the high Lord of Tuglan.

'The dominion of the eight planets extends greetings to the Arkonides, the masters of the universe,' he said in the widely understood interstellar language of the empire. 'Everything has been readied for your arrival. May I lead the way?'

A deep furrow appeared on Khrest's high forehead. He was obviously startled by the friendly reception. Rhodan on the other hand took it for granted that this was the way colonial races would welcome the rulers of the universe; he found nothing unusual in this greeting.

Rhodan's hand unconsciously stroked his white hair that contributed to his appearance as an Arkonide albino. He said slowly: 'Fly slowly ahead of us; we'll follow you!'

But the Tuglanian did not seem satisfied with this brief reply. 'You arrive just at the right moment, sir. The commissioner of Tuglan needs your help. Criminal elements destroyed the hyperwave station last night. The perpetrators were both killed.'

Khrest's forehead was smooth again. At last the situation seemed to become normal in his eyes. The battle started. How often had he encountered similar situations on other planets! The only question was who was behind the rising dissatisfaction with the Arkonide masters this time.

He would have to find out. He gave an imperceptible sign to Rhodan.

'That's why we've come here,' answered Rhodan calmly, as if this represented nothing new to him. 'Make sure that I'll be able to talk to the high commissioner immediately after our touchdown. We're short of time.'

The Tuglanian on the videoscreen nodded his head, then he disappeared.

Rhodan checked to see that the speaker was turned off before he addressed Khrest. 'Who was that?'

'I'm convinced it was the high Lord of Tuglan in person. He mentioned a rebellion, Rhodan. Against our will, you've now become a representative of the Arkonide empire! A kind of a dress rehearsal for later. What does it feel like to be in that role?'

Rhodan smiled and wondered how the red eyes would look on him. His lean frame was well-suited to play the role of an Arkonide. His heavy-set friend Reginald Bell, however, cut a rather ridiculous figure as a native of Arkon.

'If that was the Lord of Tuglan, as you say, I must

confess that I foresee some difficulties. He impressed me as being quite unsympathetic.'

'Don't come to any rash conclusions, Perry,' warned Khrest. 'The first impression must not necessarily always be right, particularly when you're dealing with an alien race. I admit, the Tuglanians resemble our own race, but they're different in some ways. To judge them by their exterior would be unfair. We must hold back our final judgment.'

Haggard and Manoli entered the Command Center, both with white hair and red eyes. They, too, were supposed to impress the Tuglanians as Arkonides. Only John Marshall had not been made up as an Arkonide albino. He would identify himself as the inhabitant of a distant solar system that only recently had become part of the galactic empire.

Marshall was not alone when he came into the Command Center. He led little Emby by the hand. The Vagabondian had undergone a session in hypno-training under Thora's supervision. With the help of complicated electronic devices it was possible to school any susceptible brain during the course of a few hours in the accumulated knowledge of generations. Therefore nobody was surprised when the mouse-beaver started talking with a squeaky voice in the language of the galactic empire:

'*Teska vyt, jenmen.*' And in English he translated: 'Good evening, gentlemen. I've also mastered the provincial language.'

Bell was so amused by the talking animal that he forgave it all its mischievous tricks – even the bath in the water kettle. He laughed until tears came into his eyes, then he bent down to the mouse-beaver to shake hands.

'Welcome, my little friend. Let's make peace!'

Emby bared his famous single incisor. 'If you'll let me play again.'

Bell lifted a warning index finger. 'Someday you can play as much as you like. But not as long as we're on this ship. It's too dangerous. Will you promise not to play here on the *Stardust*?'

'But when may I play again?' squeaked the Vagabondian miserably.

'After we've landed on Tuglan. There you'll find plenty to amuse yourself with. Now, keep quiet, we have to discuss important things.'

Emby nodded his head in an almost human gesture and sat in his corner on his broad backside. His clever eyes took everything in that went on around him.

The three Tuglanian battleships had reversed their direction meanwhile and hurried on ahead. The eleventh planet of the blue sun was visible off to the side and gradually moved into view in the frontal vid-grid. Rhodan seized the opportunity in the meantime to compare the data obtained through Khrest from the ship's colonial index file with his own current observations on the spot. Nothing seemed to have changed.

Tuglan's atmosphere was quite similar to that of Earth, with almost the same gravitational pull, just slightly higher. There were two continents in the immense ocean which covered most of the planet's surface. There was a narrow landbridge connecting the two land masses. The mountains were moderately high, gradually giving way to giant plains covered by woods. No large cities existed, for Tuglan was an agrarian society. Its technology was limited to the construction of spaceships, which kept the main planet of the Laton system in touch with the rest of the lesser planets. The Tuglanian spaceships had not yet accomplished flight at speeds faster than light. Thus the Tuglanians were unable to leave their own solar system.

It was not astonishing, therefore, that Tuglan possessed a spaceport of tremendous size despite its lack of industrial installations otherwise. The spaceport was large enough to accommodate with ease three spacespheres the size of the *Stardust*.

The three cruisers of the Tuglanians landed off to one side, standing vertically on their tail ends. Rhodan steered the *Stardust* over the center of the field and let it descend to the ground. He envisaged what impression the gigantic sphere of glittering metal would make on alien races, who would not even be able to imagine what fearsome weapons were aboard the spacecraft. Resting on the ground, the *Stardust* soared up to a height of over eight hundred yards. A sphere with a diameter of eight hundred yards! The *Stardust* was not a simple spaceship any longer – she was a small, hollow, self-contained *world*, where generations could be born and die.

One single manipulation sufficed to switch off the automatic steering system. The positronic robot installations stopped, the humming and the vibrations died down. The *Stardust* had finished her voyage.

At least for the time being.

Tuglan was just a way station, an intermission on their seemingly unending search for the planet of immortality – perhaps Tuglan would offer them a respite for a while.

But even the eternally optimistic Bell doubted that their stay with the Tuglanians would be a rest cure for the *Stardust* and her crew.

FIVE

PLOTS AND COUNTERPLOTS

Rathon, the high commissioner of the Arkonides on Tuglan, pointed with resignation at the destroyed installation of the hyperwave station.

'The very instant that you established communication with us, the bombs exploded here. One of my robots was damaged but it's been repaired meanwhile. Two Tuglanians planted the bomb and were killed while trying to escape. Unfortunately for us, for this way we couldn't find out who sent them on this mission.'

'Any clues?' inquired Khrest, and threw a quick glance to Rhodan. 'There are supposed to be some resistance groups on Tuglan, as we learned yesterday from Lord Alban. He's also quite suspicious of his younger brother Daros. To judge by Alban's hints, Daros is regarding himself already as the successor of the present ruler. It would be logical therefore if he tries to discredit his brother in our eyes.'

Rathon thoughtfully moved his head from side to side. 'I heard other tales. A few hours before the bombing attack I was informed by an unknown man that Lord Alban himself is planning an attempt on my life. He wants, so my informant told me, to free himself from our rule.'

'One accuses the other,' said Rhodan impatiently. 'How can we ever find out who speaks the truth? Where is

Daros? Why does he hide?'

'Perhaps because he has a bad conscience.'

Rhodan did not reply. He examined the radio installation which could not be repaired without the technical equipment of the *Stardust*. Chance had come to his assistance. Now it would be completely impossible for Khrest and Thora to communicate with Arkon, which, of course, they could have done directly from the *Stardust*. Much more important, though, Rathon could not send a report to Arkon, where they would be very astonished to hear of a punitive expedition of the Arkonides that had never been dispatched by them!

Rathon resumed. 'A few days ago I sent a faithful and devoted Tuglanian called Ror to Alban's palace, to make sure that all the rumors were unsubstantiated. Ror hasn't been seen since.'

'Why don't you inquire after him in the palace?' Khrest wanted to know.

The commissioner proved that he still had a spark of common sense left. 'I didn't want to give myself away. An unknown person warned me against Lord Alban, therefore, officially I should have no inkling that Alban plans a rebellion against Arkon.'

'I can't believe this story is true,' said Khrest. 'And I definitely don't think that Alban was behind any rebellion. He himself has members of the rebel movement arrested constantly and has them executed. As I was told, he's proceeding with great severity. Would he do that if he were in favor of a revolt?'

Rathon shrugged his shoulders.

'Aren't you keeping in touch with your confidential messenger?' asked Rhodan reproachfully. 'Some electronic device perhaps?'

'Robot Number Two wears a receiver that is attuned to a tiny transmitter, a mini-probe inserted in a muscle of his leg, capable of sending signals regarding his heartbeat. We might determine the direction from where the signal is coming, but not the distance. I can check up at any moment if Ror is still alive.'

'You certainly didn't overexert yourself for your own man,' Khrest blamed the commissioner. 'By the way – in which direction is Ror located now?'

Rathon motioned to RN2, who had accompanied them. 'Report about Ror, Number Two!' he commanded the robot.

The robot reacted at once. 'The receiver registers increased heart rate of the sender. Direction – over there.'

All looked to where the robot's outstretched arm was pointing. In the distance they could recognize the shining roofs of the palace. Ror was still in the palace, then, and he was also alive.

Rhodan was just about to make a remark but the robot began to announce in its monotonous voice: 'Heart beat irregular ... regular again ... skipping beats ... same direction as before ... heart stops ... no more signals ... the transmitter is silent.'

Rathon's face was deathly pale. His helpless eyes looked at Rhodan. Khrest stared sombrely at the robot. One minute ... two minutes ...

'No more signals coming through,' reported RN2.

The commissioner breathed deeply. 'Ror is dead,' he whispered softly. 'He must have died in the palace. Is that sufficient proof of Alban's involvement?'

'Not at all,' countered Rhodan. 'It could be just as well proof for the contrary. Somebody might have killed your man inside the palace in order to throw suspicion on the Lord. Maybe they discovered the transmitter probe and recognized the significance of the instrument. No, Rathon, if Alban should indeed be guilty, we'd need other means to expose him as a traitor.'

Rhodan swung around abruptly and went to the little gate leading to the street. RN2 waited there for him with the typical Tuglanian means of transport, a car with two wheels and a gravity gyroscope.

Alban had been clever enough to change his plans. Daros found out about it with great distress.

He inhabited a small apartment in a wing of the palace. From his windows he had been able to observe the landing of the huge Arkonide cruiser. He was glad to see the rulers of the mighty galactic empire. They had come to bring law and order to Tuglan. And it was just at the right moment, Daros thought to himself.

It would be unwise to rush to the spaceport and warn the Arkonides. They would never believe him. The responsibility for maintaining peace with the empire rested with Alban – and so far the peace had not been broken. And even if it had been broken, there was no proof who was to blame. It would be a very difficult task to expose the true intentions of his treacherous older brother.

And the commissioner, Rathon? One could not rely on him, for he spent his life in a dream, happy not to be bothered with Tuglanian affairs. No, he would not be of any help in the fight for justice.

Who else could be of assistance to him?

Daros came to the painful realization that he had no allies. The Tuglanians in general were not too interested in politics, and even if they should secretly sympathize with the rebels, they had no idea who the leader of the rebels was. No one had the faintest notion that the great Lord himself was planning this rebellion.

Not until independence had been gained would Alban reveal himself as the instigator and permit himself to be acclaimed as the victorious hero of his people. But in case the revolt should fail, Daros could be made the scapegoat.

Daros was shocked to the core when he became aware of his brother's cunning and maliciousness in laying a trap for him.

He felt he had to get out of the confines of the palace, that seemed more like a prison to him now. A walk through the streets would do him good and maybe clear his head. Ever since his last conversation with Alban he had known that they were enemies, mortal foes. Only one of them could survive the visit of the Arkonides: this would be the victor and thus the ruler over the realm of the eight planets.

Daros thought for a moment. Then he opened a drawer of his table and took out a small, dangerous looking pistol, known as a needler. Compressed gas was used to shoot tiny poisoned needles. The slightest touch on a person's skin was enough to paralyze any attacker.

He put the weapon in his pocket and left the palace wing.

Nobody stopped him on his way out. More than once did Daros have an uncertain feeling of being watched by invisible eyes – but it might be just his imagination. Could he have started seeing ghosts already? How could he guess, though, that Alban had given definite instructions to his allies?

There was heavy traffic in the streets. The Tuglanians were on their way to the spaceport to welcome the Arkonide masters. They had overcome their initial shock and relied on Alban's proclamation that the Arkonides were coming as friends.

Daros smiled bitterly. Anther dirty trick of his brother. He was pulling the wool over the rulers' eyes! How could they possibly still assume a rebellion had been planned if the Tuglanians seemed so happy about their arrival and greeted them with joy? If ever anyone had thought of throwing off the yoke of the Arkonide masters, it could have been only a very small minority, which now had withdrawn from view, fearing the wrath of the people and punishment from the Lord.

No, decided Daros – better not show himself at the spaceport. Wiser to wait and see. What good would it do to risk any unnecessary danger?

Tugla was a far-flung city with small houses and many gardens. A river divided the town into two parts. Nearby were some wooded hills where Daros often had gone hunting with his brother. That was quite some time ago when their father had been the Lord of Tuglan.

These mountains and woods reminded him of the carefree days of his youth. Then Alban's mind had not yet been poisoned by his greed for power and the fear of losing it again. They had been pals, good friends who shared everything alike.

Daros hailed a gyrocar. The driver pulled up and opened the door.

'Where to, sir?'

'Drive out of the city – to the mountains. Drive slowly.'

The Tuglanian shook his head. He could not understand the strange order his fare had given him: now, when everybody streamed to greet the Arkonides, this man wanted to take a leisurely drive to the mountains! Well, it was none of his business, after all, he comforted himself.

Soon they had left the city behind. It was a good road, and they rapidly picked up speed. Daros had been aware for quite a while that they were being followed.

Two other gyrocars kept at a steady distance behind them. This could not be mere coincidence. So, Alban had him under surveillance! Let him have his fun. Daros would go out of his way to avoid doing anything against Alban – as long as he lacked irrefutable evidence of his brother's evil plans.

They entered the woods. The road narrowed to a winding path as they approached the mountains. They crossed a river; afterward, the road became quite steep. Daros looked back and noticed that the two other cars had disappeared from view. Somehow this did not agree with the theory he had worked out. Had they turned back? It did not make sense.

They continued for a short stretch, then he asked the driver to stop and wait for him; he walked toward a clearing in the woods. Here he could find peace and bring order to his inner turmoil. The fresh air felt good.

Daros wandered about aimlessly for almost an hour before he decided he had better return. He would have preferred staying here, for nothing tempted him to go back to the palace.

On their way back, as they neared the river, they were held up by a road block. A tree trunk had fallen across the road. Several cars were waiting to pass. Several Tuglanians were excitedly talking but stopped when Daros got out of his car. The men broke out in smiles and then, suddenly, one of them shouted enthusiastically: 'Daros! Long live Lord Daros and the freedom of Tuglan!'

The bystanders joined in his jubilant cries and soon

the woods reverberated from their excited voices:

'Down with Lord Alban and the Arkonides! Long live Lord Daros, our liberator!'

For a few moments Daros did not understand what had gotten into these people. They seemed to have gone insane; there was no other explanation for this mad scene. He tried to fend off the overly enthusiastic men, who almost smothered him as they were tightly clustering around. He barely managed to escape to the safety of his car. Soon the tree trunk was moved out of the way and his car started off, accompanied by the cheering and applause of the crowd that had gathered around. Even later, when they had reached the city again, he could hear the shouts:

'Down with Lord Alban and his friends, the Arkonides! Long live our liberator Daros!'

Daros was suddenly seized by an overwhelming feeling of fear.

Rhodan remained skeptical.

He disliked Rathon's attempt to place the Lord of Tuglan in a bad light in his eyes. Perhaps the high commissioner of the Arkonides was simply trying to cover up his own weakness with this manoeuvre. For what interest could Alban derive from a change in the present situation?

Nevertheless...

Together with Bell, he had himself announced at the Lord's palace on the third day after the landing. The guards saluted respectfully and – as Rhodan assumed – in awe of the Arkonides. They all seemed to feel a fear in their bones of the horrible weapons in the gigantic sphere.

Alban was friendly as usual.

Courteously, he led his visitors into a small hall, which served as a reception room for diplomatic occasions.

Alban pointed to three chairs.

'Have a seat, please. To what do I owe the honor of your visit, noble Arkonides? May I inquire if you are satisfied so far with your mission that brought you to our planet?'

Rhodan remained standing.

'Who's the leader of the opposition against the galactic empire?' he asked abruptly. 'What's the size of this resistance group, what are their goals and who's behind this movement?'

Alban cringed for an instant, then shook his head with exaggerated sadness. 'Noble lords, I've been afraid that you might bring up this question. But believe me, I can easily handle this affair. I don't wish to bother you with such trifles. I'm the Lord of Tuglan and I shall punish anybody who dares to insult the empire.'

'I still want to know who is the leader of these rebels,' insisted Rhodan. 'Some people have claimed it's your own brother.'

Alban lowered his eyes with embarrassment. Then with surprising frankness he looked straight at Rhodan.

'That's absolute nonsense, noble Arkonide. I'd stake my life on my brother's integrity. He's not involved at all in this resistance movement.'

Rhodan was surprised; he had counted on a different reaction from Alban – that he would seize this opportunity to incriminate his brother Daros. The rumors he had heard were apparently not correct. Rathon must obviously be mistaken to consider Alban a conniver.

'I'd like to meet your brother,' said Rhodan.

Alban nodded obligingly and motioned to one of the

servants. Hardly two minutes later, a young Tuglanian entered the room, hesitated for a moment at the door on seeing the two presumed Arkonides; then he slowly started to move forward. His eyes were fixed on Rhodan all the time. He ignored Alban's presence.

An undecided character, thought Rhodan. He seemed to be unsure of himself. Bad conscience? Or something else that worried him?

He decided to ask the young man directly. 'I'm Rhodan, the commander of the surveillance expedition. This is my deputy.' He pointed at Bell, who proudly stuck out his chest. 'Rumors are going around that there's a strong opposition here on Tuglan desiring independence from Arkon and the galactic empire. The bombing attack on our local radio installation proves that this isn't idle talk on their part. I was told that you're involved in this organization. Will you please explain how it's possible that you could be accused of this?'

Daros briefly glanced at Alban with contempt.

'It's a lie!' he said firmly. 'My brother's a liar. He's the one who wants independence from Arkon. He himself has been the instigator of the attack against the broadcast station. His men perished trying to flee from the robots. He had even planned the murder of Commissioner Rathon, but, fortunately, you arrived just in time to prevent this. I know that my brother wants to make me look suspicious so that I'll become the scapegoat for his own misdeeds. He's afraid I desire to become his successor. He wants to eliminate me.'

Rhodan scrutinized the young man. He was startled by this outburst. Although Daros impressed him far more favorably in general than Alban, the older brother, nevertheless, had avoided casting aspersions on his younger brother's character. On the contrary, he had defended him. This spoke in his favor. Daros, on the other hand, had brought severe accusations against Alban.

How could this be explained? Who was to be believed? Rhodan regretted not having brought John Marshall along with him. The telepath would have correctly sized up the situation at once. No lies would get by him.

Alban, his face contorted with a woeful smile, shook his head. 'Oh, Daros, how reckless of you! I wanted to spare you and concealed your treacherous activities from the noble Arkonides. Now, however, since you've chosen to attack me, I'm forced to defend myself.' He beckoned to one of the silently waiting servants. 'Fortunately, I have my men everywhere. They've secretly kept you under surveillance, Daros. And recently, when you met your rebel friends, they obtained concrete evidence of your conspiracy. Here, noble Arkonides, see and hear for yourselves!'

He pushed a button and the curtains closed. It grew almost dark in the reception hall. In the front of the room, a ground glass screen began to glow softly, then the three-dimensional and true-to-life image of a bridge over a river could be seen. A large crowd surrounded a car. A young Tuglanian was standing next to the car. The people were shouting jubilantly, hailing and cheering the young man, constantly repeating their request:

'Down with Alban and his friends, the Arkonides! Long live Lord Daros, our liberator!'

Rhodan recognized immediately that the young Tuglanian on the three-dimensional screen was none other than Daros himself. The rebel leader with his followers. Was there any more convincing proof?

Still, Rhodan was sorry to witness this demonstration

of the young man's guilt. But emotions had to be set aside, here, where the supremacy of the Arkonides was at stake. Leniency meant weakness in this case. And weakness equaled downfall and decadence.

'Daros, I regret but I have to place you under arrest. The empire cannot permit any acts of rebellion. Lord Alban, we're sorry but we have to take your brother in custody. We will put him in our temporary prison on board the *Stardust*.'

'If it has to be this way, I cannot object to his imprisonment under the circumstances,' replied Alban; then he turned to Daros and asked, 'Why did you accuse me? I had no alternative but to defend myself.'

'You traitor!' snarled Daros. 'I'm ready,' he announced to Rhodan. 'May the day come soon enough for you to forgive yourself for the mistake you're making. Before it's too late.'

Without further words, Rhodan and Bell left the room with their prisoner.

Alban stared after them unflinchingly. There was just a hint of triumph in his hard eyes.

Somewhere in a spacious basement the rebels gathered. But there were no rebels against the Arkonide empire; they were the Tuglanians who did not agree with Alban's insidious politics. They desired no changes in the present power structure. They only wished to preserve the status quo. Daros had been chosen by them to become the new Lord, for he would be a guarantee that Tuglan would remain part of the mighty empire.

Daros knew nothing about them, since he was no revolutionary. He had no idea that his brother had many enemies who wanted to remove him from power and who planned to replace him by Daros.

Among the assembled in the basement were some adventurous types, and many others who pursued an honest trade, respected citizens. Others, though, lived in the woods and remained in hiding, waiting for the signal for the revolt. They carried arms and were fully prepared to use them, for Alban had threatened all traitors with death – a threat to be taken seriously, for if the tyrant was not afraid to execute his own followers for the sake of appearances, he would not hesitate a single moment to mercilessly kill his personal enemies.

A man entered the basement through a back door. He was short-set, almost corpulent, but his movements revealed an amazing agility. His violet, shiny hair was combed straight back and imparted a demoniacal expression to his features. It was easy to imagine that his appearance alone was enough to infuse the crowds with enthusiasm.

As the rebels caught sight of him they began to murmur softly in unison:

'Long live the new Lord Daros! Long live the empire of the Arkonides! Long live the revolution against Alban, the traitor!'

The new arrival raised both hands in an imploring gesture.

'I, Karolan, the leader of the Just Cause, have to report something of importance to you. The day of freedom is near but we still face the great task of proving Alban's guilt. The cunning traitor has managed to make Daros suspect in the eyes of the Arkonide mission. They've arrested Daros. What's our next move?'

A hushed silence fell over the crowd, which received the news with dismay. Then all began to talk excitedly at the same time. Not a word could be understood, until someone from the back of the room shouted over the din of the voices: 'Free Daros! Let's free him!'

Karolan shook his head.

'That would be a mistake, friends. It would only reinforce the suspicion surrounding him. We could do no greater favor to Alban than to liberate Daros. This would be conclusive proof in the eyes of the Arkonides, and we'd have to expect reprisals. No, friends, there must be a better solution, a more diplomatic way.'

'Let's send a delegation to the Arkonides,' suggested another man.

'That sounds better, but who can guarantee that they'll believe us? Most likely, Alban's already foreseen that we might resort to such tactics, and he's already laid the groundwork to sow doubt in the minds of the Arkonides about our credibility. His talent for intrigues is unsurpassed, as you know.'

'Very true,' replied a slender man who had pushed to the fore. 'Alban knows about us, but he's misrepresented our aims to the Arkonides. He says we're against him – and up to this point he's speaking the truth and no lie detector could expose him. But he passes over in silence that we are *for* the empire. And as long as he remains silent, it'll be difficult to prove his untruthfulness.'

'I have an idea...' began Karolan, but he was interrupted. A man rushed through the main entrance door and elbowed his way through the crowd, ruthlessly pushing people aside until he stood before the leader of the rebels. His chest was heaving violently as if he had been running a long way without stop. Pearls of perspiration beaded his forehead. Several times he tried to speak but he failed to utter a sound. Totally exhausted, he permitted some of his friends to support him.

Karolan frowned. 'What's the matter, Xaron?'

'Daros! The Arkonides have placed him under arrest in the palace, and now, they've taken him to their spacesphere.'

That's no news to us, Xaron. Did you rush here to tell us warmed-over news?'

'But you don't know that Daros was freed on the way to the spacesphere. Ten masked men ambushed the two Arkonides and Daros. And most strange – the two Arkonides did not put up any resistance. They permitted themselves to be taken prisoner and dargged off in a gyrocar that quickly took off from there. Daros wasn't even handcuffed!'

Karolan remained silent for a long time. Deep furrows marked his forehead. Then he said: 'Alban wants to intensify Daros' guilt even further. He's clever. But the Arkonides are far more clever than he is. They realize that nothing untoward will befall them, for their companions' vengeance would be terrible. Therefore they let the ten men do what they wanted in order to find out what's behind all this. It doesn't surprise me any longer that they built up an empire and ruled over it for so long. But let us not underestimate Alban. I'd bet that he's already prepared his next coup.'

None of the men present in the basement realized how right Karolan was with his conjecture.

The situation seemed rather odd.

While Rhodan, Bell and Daros were on their way back to the *Stardust*, their way was suddenly blocked by ten masked Tuglanians. Resolutely, Bell drew his ray gun, ready to defend himself and his two companions. No doubt it would have been easy game to overcome the poorly armed bandits, but Rhodan raised his hand.

'Don't, Reg. This wouldn't bring us any nearer our actual goal. We must know who sent them and what their plans are. If necessary, let them take us prisoner. Do nothing reckless!'

Bell pushed the weapon back into his holster. 'As you say, Perry, but I think you're making a mistake. This will undermine our authority.'

'That's not so important right now.'

The car stopped. The masked men crowded around and pulled the doors open.

'Long live Daros, our new Lord! Down with the Arkonides!'

Daros was probably the one who could understand the least what was happening. He cowered, frightened and helpless, next to Bell. He had no idea who these people might be who had come to rescue him from the Arkonides. What puzzled him most, however, was the Arkonides' reaction – why did they not put up any resistance?

Rhodan and Bell were dragged from their car and disarmed. Daros, on the other hand, was politely asked to step out of the car and to come along. Hastily, the two prisoners, and the 'liberated' Daros were led down the street and placed in a waiting truck. The windowless cabin was shut and the vehicle started to move. The three men had no idea what their destination might be.

The ten kidnappers conversed in their own language. To his amazement, Rhodan noticed that he could understand almost everything and it was quite a shock to realize that the Tuglanians spoke an Arkonide dialect. Why hadn't Khrest told him anything about this? Was he himself even aware of it?

Rhodan scrutinized the men. They had removed their

masks but this was not of much help. He did not know any of them. The conversation dealt with trivia. Probably they did not want Daros to find out anything about them.

This, on the other hand, reinforced Rhodan's suspicions. He was convinced that Alban's younger brother was totally ignorant as to whom he owed his freedom. Otherwise he certainly would have behaved differently. Daros was a prisoner, the same as Rhodan and Bell, with one exception only: he had not been handcuffed.

They drove for nearly half an hour, then the car came to a sudden halt. The door was yanked open and the kidnappers pushed their prisoners into a half-dark room. The air was very close.

One of the Tuglanians approached Daros, bowed before him and said in Pankosmo:

'We're overjoyed, Lord Daros, to have liberated you from the hands of the Arkonides. May I ask you to accompany us, please.'

Daros glanced at Rhodan, an insecure expression in his eyes, but before he could manage to open his mouth to reply, he was gently but forcibly conducted out of the room. He had no time to thank his liberators – or to protest against this abduction.

Rhodan was fully convinced now that he had witnessed a put-on act.

An antigrav elevator brought him, Bell and several Tuglanians farther down below, then they were locked up in a cell which contained nothing but two beds and a table. Soon the steps of the unknown kidnappers faded away in the corridor outside their cell.

Bell stared at the heavy planks of the wooden door, sighed and sat down on the nearest bed. From the ceiling, a lamp dimly illuminated the small room.

'A pretty kettle of fish! Do you really believe they'll let go of us again? I wonder what they'll do to Daros.'

'Put him in a cell, just like us,' answered Rhodan. 'And – don't worry, Reg, at least one of us will be set free, for how else will the Arkonides find out that Daros was liberated by his political friends?'

'Are you sure?'

'Absolutely! Alban's clever enough. But its probably wiser not to talk so much. The walls might have ears.'

Bell stretched out on the bed. 'In such a situation it's always the smartest thing to go to sleep.'

Slowly and thoughtfully, Rhodan nodded his head in agreement.

Two hours later they came to fetch Bell.

To a hearing, they said. Rhodan remained alone in the cell. He guessed that Alban had started to make his next move.

Bell's handcuffs were not removed. He was placed in a small two-wheeled vehicle. Besides the driver another armed rebel sat in the car. Then the car passed through a big gate out into the street and mingled in the traffic.

Bell tried to remember the way but he soon lost his sense of orientation. The car drove through busy streets, then quieter suburbs. Once Bell thought they had crossed the same square twice. Did his abductors want to confuse him?

And then, quite close to the palace, it happened. Bell had no idea that Rhodan could have predicted this incident. But as far as Bell was concerned, this event only added to his confusion: still, he wasted no time pondering about it. The main thing was, that the car was suddenly stopped by several men in uniform. The driver and the armed guard protested loudly: then all of a sudden large energy fingers flared up and silenced them forever. One of the uniformed men opened and removed Bell's handcuffs.

'We're happy we can render this service to the noble Arkonide,' said one of them in the usual Pankosmo. 'One of our men in the palace informed us of the kidnapping and your transfer from the place where you were imprisoned. Alban has his spies everywhere, fortunately.'

'Lord Alban?' wondered Bell, and decided to change his opinion regarding the ruler of the Tuglanians. 'Do I owe my release to him?'

'None other, noble Arkonide.'

Bell was not especially thrilled to be addressed all the time as a 'noble Arkonide' – but he had to continue to pretend and to play his role, whether he liked it or not.

'Why did you kill these two men?' he wanted to know, pointing at the two bodies of his now dead abductors.

'They offered resistance.'

Bell had not noticed too much resistance. Too bad, now they could no longer be questioned as to where the prison was located in which Rhodan was still being detained. Or should they . . .

A thought flashed through Bell's mind. In connection with Rhodan's hints, it suddenly seemed to make sense.

'Lead me to Lord Alban,' he requested.

His request was carried out surprisingly fast. Ten minutes later he sat opposite the dark-haired ruler. Having had to listen too long for his taste to Alban's effusive congratulations, Bell cut him short with a commanding gesture.

'I fully appreciate your help, Lord Alban, but my commander is still in the hands of the rebels. Do you have any clues where he might be detained?'

'I'm sorry, I don't have any, noble Arkonide. My spy reported only that he saw you in the city, whereupon I alarmed my guards at once and ordered them to free you. Furthermore, I learned that my brother Daros has been rescued by the rebels. We don't know where he is at the moment. I'm afraid, though, that he will very earnestly gather his followers and prepare a revolution against the empire and me.'

'So that's it,' said Bell. 'Daros wants to overthrow your regime and separate Tuglan from the realm of the Arkonides?'

'Unfortunately, yes,' answered Alban with a sorrowful expression. 'I can't imagine what advantages he sees if Tuglan should become independent. We're faring well in our union with the realm of the Arkonides; we're enjoying many benefits by it.'

'Certainly,' nodded Bell, his thoughts meanwhile were racing ahead. 'And your brother's friends desire the revolution, if I understand you right? And they're responsible for the bombing of our radio station? And they arrested Rhodan and myself? Have they also liberated Daros?'

With every question Alban's nodding became increasingly eager. His eyes were shining with joy.

'I see you've grasped the situation. If you wish peace and order on Tuglan you must find Daros.'

'First of all, I want to find Rhodan,' grumbled Bell. 'By the way, where's Commissioner Rathon now?'

'He went on board your spaceship.'

Bell rose from his chair. 'Thanks again for your help. I believe now the incident at the radio station was caused by the action of a relatively small group of rebels. Collective punishment of Tuglan won't be necessary under the circumstances. Of course, if our Commander Rhodan shouldn't reappear very soon...'

Alban leaned forward, his eyes shining with cunning. 'What then? Will you wipe out the rebels?'

Bell shook his head. 'Not just the rebels, Alban. All of Tuglan! We can't allow ourselves to make any mistakes. It's better to wipe out an entire solar system than set a poor example for weak colonial governments. I hope you understand that.'

Just as Bell walked out of the room and closed the door behind him, he threw a swift glance over his shoulder. He felt great satisfaction at the sight of Alban's frightened face.

Bell had never before seen Khrest at a complete loss but this time the Arkonide scientist seemed to have reached the end of his tether. With Rhodan gone, nothing remained of his usual display of superiority, and even Thora showed signs of uncertainty, although with Rhodan's death their chances to return to their home planet Arkon would finally increase. After all, the two Arkonides had concluded a pact with Rhodan and not with Bell, a pact which obligated them to first find the planet of eternal life before returning to their world thirty-four thousand light-years from Earth.

'And you couldn't find the way again?' Khrest made sure once more. 'The prison's in Tugla: it shouldn't be so difficult to locate again! I can't understand it.'

'If you'd been along on this crazy drive you'd understand it. Back and forth and roundabout, one street looking exactly like the other. But I'm dead sure that sly Alban knows exactly where Rhodan's imprisoned. Maybe the whole affair was masterminded by him.'

'By Alban? I can't believe it.'

'It seems most unlikely, but still. We should make sure of his real intentions and send a telepath to him who'd soon find out whether he's speaking the truth when questioned.'

'You mean John Marshall?'

'Yes, why not? We should have done this quite some time ago, then we'd know at least who wants to overthrow whom and introduce a new order.' Bell looked suddenly as if searching for something. 'Where's Emby?'

Khrest seemed taken aback. 'Emby? The mouse-beaver?'

'Yes. I wonder where he might be.' Bell's voice sounded anxious. 'I'm worried if I don't know where that little guy is.'

'Are you so fond of that animal?' inquired Thora sarcastically.

'That's partially it. But first of all I'm bothered by what I promised him before we landed.'

'What was it?' asked Khrest.

'That he could play to his heart's content. Just imagine all the things he can find here in Tugla to amuse himself with . . .'

Bell asked Marshall to accompany Khrest to the Lord's palace. Then he went to search for Emby.

Ten minutes later he knew that the mouse-beaver was no longer on board the Arkonide battleship.

SIX

THE MIND READER'S REVELATION

Several things happened simultaneously.

Khrest, accompanied by the telepath John Marshall and Rathon, the Arkonide high commissioner, went to the palace of the ruling Lord of the Tuglanians and asked to see him.

Bell gave up the fruitless search for Emby and went to see Wuriu Sengu, the mutant. The hefty Japanese was the 'seer' of the mutant corps. His eyes could penetrate solid matter and recognize any object hidden behind it from ordinary sight. Unfortunately, his talents were still limited to a certain distance. Nevertheless, Bell was confident enough of Sengu's abilities to have him accompany him while roaming the streets of Tugla. The Japanese tried as hard as he could to locate Rhodan somewhere in any of the innumerable buildings of the town.

In the meantime, however, Rhodan was taken by car from the place where he had been imprisoned to the palace of the Lord. In a cellar dungeon he found his abode for the time being. Rhodan was firmly convinced that Alban would soon let his mask fall. He did not fear for his life as yet.

Daros, too, landed in prison, in the same place as Rhodan – in fact, just a few yards away from him. Neither of the two knew of the other's presence, however, Alban's brother had a clear idea who kept him imprisoned but he did not comprehend how involved a plot was behind all this. For Daros, complicated moves, as in a game of chess, meant cumbersome detours without rhyme or reason. If he had been in Alban's place, he would have acted swiftly and straightforwardly.

Only the fifth event had not been planned for.

It was easy for Emby to leave the ship unnoticed. Everybody knew who he was and therefore did not challenge him. On the gangway, one of the space-fighter pilots bent down to him and scratched him behind the ear.

'Well, fellow, going for a walk?'

The mouse-beaver nodded his head seriously. 'I'm not permitted to play inside the ship,' he said in a squeaky voice. Then he chirped, filled with joyous anticipation. 'But now my time for playing has finally come – but only outside the ship. There are lots of things for me to play with, I was told.'

'As long as you leave our ship in peace, nobody will mind,' warned the pilot with a raised forefinger. 'And watch out for the Tuglanians, Emby. Not all are friends.'

'Don't worry,' twittered Emby, merrily rolling his big round eyes, 'I'm not afraid of them.'

'Stay close to the ship,' was the pilot's final advice, while his eyes followed the droll creature who, now fully erect, waddled down the moving escalator. Unfortunately, the pilot had missed Bell's inquiry over the ship's intercom; therefore it did not occur to him to report this encounter with Emby to anyone.

The mouse-beaver, on the other hand, had not the slightest intention of remaining close to the ship. He walked leisurely toward the buildings at the edge of the spaceport, then teleported over a barrier and found himself on the road leading to town. For a while he stood there, admiring everything, and observed with great interest all the many little cars driving back and forth, depositing and picking up passengers. These little vehicles would make splendid toys! But it would probably be better to play with those that were unoccupied. Those two-legged creatures were peculiar in many ways and showed little understanding for real fun.

In the nearby parking lot, Emby finally found what he had been desperately searching for. The employees of the spaceport had parked their cars there. There they stood, in long rows, idle and apparently not in use.

At least that was the way it seemed to Emby. He was determined to take care of that situation.

And while he waddled merrily down the street leading to the faraway city, five of the parked cars moved out of the long rows and, without the usual hum of motors, slid smoothly onto the road, formed a column and rolled leisurely along, at walking speed, keeping just ahead of Emby.

This unusual parade did not remain unnoticed for long. Cars approaching from the opposite direction moved out of the way hastily to avoid a collision. The occupants of those cars were driving at high speed so that they had no time to notice any irregularity. But it was a different story for those cars that overtook the strange column.

They had ample time to observe the obstacle in their way and they noticed at once that the five gyrocars traveled along without any drivers. They seemed to be guided by spirit hands, kept in perfect formation as they leisurely proceeded toward town. That was, to say the least, most unusual.

Emby, himself, was an unusual sight, but people paid

little attention to him. Although there was hardly any more interstellar trade these days, people still remembered the long bygone times when frequently the most peculiar creatures had landed on Tuglan. The great empire was composed of many different races. Today, as everybody knew, a big battleship of the Arkonide Empire had arrived at the spaceport. Besides the Arkonides, there were probably some representatives of their colonial empire aboard. This odd little fellow must be one of them, but it would not have occurred to any Tuglanian to connect the driverless column of cars with the little mouse-beaver.

Emby, meanwhile, enjoyed himself tremendously.

But not for very long. The evenly rolling vehicles soon became a bit boring.

Emby displayed his single incisor with a friendly, mischievous grin, and gave his brain a command. The same instant, the police cars, which meanwhile had been alerted, experienced quite a surprise.

They had received orders to stop this ghostly procession. But instead of stopping, the five gyrocars rose effortlessly into the air and soon reached a height of fifty yards. There they executed some fancy manoeuvres, all the time remaining in perfect alignment, and even looped some risky loops.

As long as they had lived, the poor bewildered policemen had never seen flying motorcars. Tuglan's technology was quite advanced, admittedly; they had spaceships flying at tremendous speeds, rocketships, but no flying gyrocars.

Traffic on the wide street threatened to turn into chaos. Vehicles stopped and a traffic jam developed. The drivers got out of their gyrocars in order to watch the miracle of the machines floating up in the air. Only Emby kept marching on. People still did not pay attention to him but he had hopes that maybe the townspeople might be a bit smarter and admire his tricks.

Soon he got tired of playing with the five cars and withdrew his thoughts from them, all the while toddling along toward town.

Promptly, the five cars fell to the ground. But, luckily, Emby had made them perform their tricks a little to the side of the road, so that they crashed into a field where they were totally demolished. Policemen and civilians ran to the scene of the crashed vehicles to make sure that no Tuglanian was buried under the debris. They still had no idea how these driverless cars could have risen into the air.

Emby wandered calmly on. It took him half an hour to reach the outskirts of the city but he caused such havoc in this brief span of time that news of these inexplicable incidents reached as far as the palace where Alban was just getting ready to receive Khrest and Marshall.

Gyrocars no longer obeyed their drivers, who were helplessly manipulating the steering mechanisms. But to their horror their cars did the exact opposite of what they were supposed to. Some vehicles simply rolled off the road and rattled over the fields lining the road until they finally came to a halt. Others, on the other hand, sailed up ahead, a few yards off the ground, only to make a rough landing somewhere along the road. Once a curiously staring policeman was struck in the back and pushed to the ground. Turning around furiously to see who his attacker might be, any word of protest got stuck in his throat. In front of him hovered one of the many trash containers that normally could be found at any street corner – but not up in the air.

The policeman swiftly recalled all his secret misdeeds and was sure that the gods wanted to punish him. He thought he had lost his mind. A trash basket might quickly fly through the air but not leisurely hover in mid-air. And morever, it would not dare attack a public servant of the state!

Slowly, the bewildered man got to his feet, his eyes fixed on the trash container. The container rose a bit and then hovered directly overhead. Then the container made a turn of exactly 180°. Its entire contents poured over the head of the pitiable policeman, who just that morning had put on a freshly pressed uniform.

Then the basket lost its hold in the air and fell down. Passersby came to the rescue of the unfortunate policeman and freed him from the tightly-looped wire basket that enclosed him like a captured animal behind a wire fence.

Emby, in the meantime, ambled on, very pleased with himself. He had quickly discovered how marvelous one could play with these harmless two-legged creatures.

Emby noticed a woman at a corner. He made her rise up and set her gently down on the roof of a house. From across the street Emby watched how people dragged tall ladders to bring her down again. Although he could have easily interfered, his attention was suddenly diverted.

Three of the dark two-legged creatures had approached him. In their hands they held the same funny-looking pistols that Rhodan and his friends would use when in danger. That meant that these guys had not very friendly intentions toward him.

'He belongs to the ship of the Arkonides,' said one of the men.

Emby was unable to understand their words directly,

but a part of his intricate brain seemed suddenly to awaken. The strange thoughts penetrated his mind and became comprehensible impulses.

'Is it an animal or an intelligent being?'

That made some sense to Emby. They thought, then, that he was an animal.

'Perhaps it's gotten away from the ship . . . ?' wondered another man, and lowered his weapon. 'Let's catch it and collect a reward.'

Well, then he wouldn't be able to play any more, thought Emby. He felt very annoyed.

'We must bring it first to Lord Alban; only he can decide what to do with it.'

Emby was, of course, somewhat informed of the whole situation. He had listened in to the conversation aboard the *Stardust*. These people, therefore, were followers of Alban.

'Be careful, men. Don't frighten him! Here, here, little fellow! Where's the cute little guy?'

Emby thought that this question was utterly stupid.

After all, they could plainly see where he was. And he was not the least bit frightened.

He stopped and eyed the men curiously. He was satisfied to see that they had put their weapons away. He must impress them as being very harmless. Although he did not like that too well, it suited him at this particular moment.

If they would behave decently, he would come along with them. Who could tell, the whole affair might turn out to be a lot of fun.

He was rather startled when the first man bent down and seized him roughly by the scruff of his neck. That hurt! And Emby reacted instinctively to defend himself.

The man felt as though grabbed by a huge fist that yanked him into the air. He saw the ground sink away from under him and the walls of the houses race downward on either side of the street. Way down below he could make out the upturned faces of his companions and their wide, staring eyes.

And then, the invisible fist let go of him. He fell and saw the street race toward him. And then –

He did not feel the impact; he died on the spot.

Emby smoothed down his ruffled fur. That brute would not grab him by the scruff of his neck anymore! With a friendly grin, baring his one and only tooth, he addressed the two remaining Tuglanians, a slight reproach in his voice: 'If you want to play with me, you mustn't touch me.'

The talking creature was the last straw! The two men lost the last shreds of their composure. It was too spooky. Especially what had happened to their companion. Automatically their hands flew to their weapons. They drew their ray guns. This animal was dangerous; it had to be put out of action. Who knew what else these Arkonides might have brought along in their spaceship!

The visitor from Vagabond watched them calmly. He gazed at the dangerous guns. The invisible energy fingers of his telekinetic brain regions penetrated the firing mechanism, disrupting important circuits.

The two men pressed the firing buttons but nothing happened. The deadly rays failed to materialize. Instead, all the metal parts of their pistols heated up tremendously, liquefied and dripped to the ground.

Cursing wildly, the men hurled their useless weapons against the wall of the nearest house; then perplexed, stared at Emby with their mouths hanging wide open.

Then they swiftly turned on their heels and ran off as fast as their legs would carry them.

The whole incident had not remained unnoticed.

From across the street, four Tuglanians hurried over, briefly examined the dead man and advanced toward Emby. One of the men said:

'It's one of Alban's men; I know him. The little guy over there killed him. It's a mystery how he did it. In any case, he doesn't seem to be very friendly toward our enemies. Why don't we ask him?'

Well, well, thought Emby. That seemed interesting. These Tuglanians seemed to be from the other party, and they appeared much nicer.

'If that little guy over there has arrived with the Arkonide spaceship he might be able to help us. He must be a member of the union of the empire.'

'You're right, Xaron. I only wonder how we can make ourselves understood.'

Emby had heard enough. These men were in trouble of some kind. Only he could help them. He would be happy to. Perhaps these men were on Daros' side?

The four Tuglanians stopped before Emby and tried a friendly grin. One of them pointed to the dead man who was still lying in the street.

'*You* did that, didn't you? Well done, friend. He was an enemy of the galactic empire.'

Emby spoke English fluently now as well as some Pankosmo – enough to make himself understood. 'Also an enemy of Perry Rhodan?'

'Who's Perry Rhodan?'

'The commander of our spaceship.'

'Of course, he was Rhodan's enemy too. We'll explain everything to you. But not now – here comes the police

... we mustn't be caught by them.'

Before the four men could take off, two or three gyro-cars tore around the corner and came to a screeching halt. Uniformed men jumped out of the cars, drawing their weapons, and ran toward Emby and his four new friends.

'Don't be scared!' chirped Emby overjoyed to be able once more to show off his tricks. 'We'll teach them a thing or two.'

And the same moment, Karolan's four men became weightless and sailed upward and toward a nearby house, where they landed on top of the flat roof. They hardly felt firm ground under their feet again, when they regained their natural weight. They could not figure out what was happening to them and why. They clung desperately to a narrow railing that separated them from the abyss below. But their curiosity exceeded their fear. Especially since most peculiar things were taking place down there on the street. It was too good to be missed. And they forgot their tragicomical situation and peered down below.

All perplexed, the policemen stared after the flying Tuglanians, but they quickly calmed down. After all, they had witnessed something similar barely half an hour earlier. Cars had been flying through the air – and the same little animal had been nearby. Now men were sailing through the air, and once again the little furry creature was present, looking as harmless as a mouse.

Suddenly it dawned on them that there must be some connection between the miracles and the little fellow.

'Get it alive!' yelled the leader of the brave troop and with a death-defying gesture he rushed toward Emby, whose big tooth danced up and down in happy anticipation. His fur bristled all over. Oh, joy! Now he could play and play! Almost more than he could handle at one time.

The policemen were seized by an invisible fist and pulled back into their gyrocars. Before they realized what was happening, they sat again in their vehicles, which set themselves in motion as if guided by mysterious spirits. The cars aligned in a smart formation and then ascended. The horrified policemen soon saw the city way down below in the depths. They crouched, perfectly still, in their cabins – they did not dare to even move a finger. The inhabitants of Tugla, however, enjoyed the spectacle of aerial acrobatics as performed by their own motorized police force. The performance lasted just two minutes, then the cars landed unharmed on the roof of the palace.

Meanwhile, Emby had jumped up to the roof with a mighty leap, there to be warmly greeted by the relieved four rebels. They still failed to comprehend how all this had been possible but they accepted Emby's magic tricks simply as another manifestation of the wonders of the almighty Arkonide realm. One more reason to go all out for remaining within this empire.

Nobody could disturb the little group up there on the roof and so they took the occasion to inform Emby about the political situation on the planet. He learned more in this short time than Rhodan had ever known about this system. Thanks to his telepathic powers Emby was able to tell that the four men were not lying.

Rhodan was in danger and captured by Alban? It was high time to liberate him!

'We'll take you to Karolan, our leader,' they said to Emby. 'He'll know what to do. You're our salvation. How can we thank you?'

Emby modestly waved aside the compliment with a

paw. 'As long as I have a chance to play, that's all I want.'

This remark did not seem too clear to the four men but they really did not care what the mouse-beaver meant by it. The main thing was, they had found a powerful ally for their cause.

And thus they started on their way to join Karolan in his hiding place.

Bell abandoned his futile search for Rhodan. He decided to set out for the palace, where Khrest and Marshall were negotiating with Lord Alban. Wuriu Sengu, the seer of the mutant corps, accompanied Bell. Sengu had been unsuccessful so far in uncovering any trace of Rhodan's whereabouts, although the solid walls of the houses presented no obstacle to his vision. Under his scrutinizing gaze the structure of solid matter changed and became transparent. Sengu was capable of regulating the exact distance to which this process extended. This way he could penetrate layer after layer until he had found what he was looking for.

But there was no trace of Rhodan, wherever he searched.

Inside the palace, there was a great deal of commotion. Bell regarded the gyrocars parked on the palace roof and wondered how they had gotten up there. A guard explained in great detail how some invisible entity had been playing tricks with the local police. Their cars had been flung through the air – and all kinds of other objects as well: guns, policemen, people...

It dawned on Bell gradually what might be behind all these magic phenomena. He remembered having failed to locate Emby anywhere on the *Stardust*. Could the playful mouse-beaver have gone on a rampage to satisfy his craze for funny games? These incidents looked suspiciously like something the little fellow might have concocted.

Where could Emby be right now?

Bell was interrupted in his speculations by the arrival of a Tuglanian in uniform who brought Alban's reply to Bell's request for an interview. The two visitors were supposed to wait until Alban's conference with the Arkonide Khrest and his companion was terminated. This was what Khrest had requested.

Bell nodded curtly and quickly exchanged a glance with Sengu. As soon as the guard was out of earshot, Bell whispered:

'Khrest wouldn't object to our presence during his talk with Lord Alban. That sounds fishy!'

The Japanese mutant pondered a moment. 'What do you suggest? Should I have a look?'

'Yes, go ahead!'

Wuriu Sengu started to activate a special region of his brain. The stone walls began to dissolve before his searching eyes and he could see through them unimpeded into the rooms lying beyond.

Bell sat beside him, inactive. He was furious to be nothing but a normal human being and not a mutant.

Lord Alban had hardly uttered a few words when it became clear to Marshall that the Tuglanian Lord was lying.

Marshall, Rathon and Khrest had been led to the Lord's reception chambers by a regular parade troop that marched them along corridors and stairways of the spacious palace. With all military honors – or under strict surveillance. Marshall was certain that the ray guns the guards presented were no trappings. He listened in briefly to the thought streams of the guard. This fully confirmed his suspicions.

Alban greeted his visitors effusively and emphasized how sorry he was to hear that the noble Arkonides were being inconvenienced. He assured them that he would see to it personally that law and order would be restored. Indeed, he suggested after a while, it might be advisable to let him proceed on his own initiative, just to leave all matters to him. Even the affair of the missing Rhodan. He was certain he would find him, wherever he might be.

Khrest noticed that Marshall shook his head slightly, but he could not make out from that at what point Alban had been lying. Alban had said too many things at one time. Perhaps it would be wiser to deal with each question individually.

'You mean to say,' Khrest asked therefore, 'that you believe your brother Daros to be plotting against the Arkonide empire?'

'He's the leader of the rebels.'

Khrest looked over to Marshall and knew that Alban had not spoken the truth.

'And he's responsible for the bombing of the high commissioner's radio station?'

'Of course, who else?'

Alban lying again.

'You, Alban, on the other hand, are a loyal subject of the galactic empire? Is it your desire that Tuglan remain within the union of our star realm as before?'

'Naturally, noble Arkonide, this is my dearest wish.'

Khrest had learned all he needed with these three questions.

Marshall, by now, was quite openly shaking his head.

Khrest no longer saw any reason why he should still hold back. True, he and Marshall had come here unarmed, but he hoped his authority would be sufficient to prevent Alban from committing any foolish acts.

'You're not telling the truth, Lord Alban,' he said bluntly, reproachfully. 'Your brother has nothing to do with this whole affair. You fear him as a rival. It was you who ordered the destruction of the radio station and, in addition, you were responsible for the ambush of Rhodan's car. Where is Rhodan? Speak the truth, Alban! Or else I'll have my crew annihilate the entire city of Tugla!'

Lord Alban sat behind his desk. He did not budge. His tightly clenched fists rested on the table top. It took long seconds before he could overcome his surprise. With a twisted smile he finally muttered:

'These are horrendous accusations, Khrest. How can you possibly prove your allegations?'

'I need no proofs. This man here is a thought-reader, Alban. He knows you were lying.'

Alban glanced at Marshall. His eyes flickered. 'A telepath? How can such a thing be?'

'There are many races in our empire and among them some capable of telepathy. Your thoughts no longer remain secret for us. Marshall, tell him what you know.'

'Alban's the one,' began Marshall, 'who wants to shake off the Arkonide rule. At the same time he wanted to eliminate his brother. For that reason he skillfully managed to cast all suspicions on Daros. He wanted to get rid of him legally and to whitewash himself at the same time. We came just in the nick of time.'

Meanwhile, Alban had pushed a secret signal button. Outside in the corridor, the hurrying steps of the approaching guards could be heard. He smiled coldly. 'What use can you make of that knowledge? How can the people of your ship find out about it?'

'What do you mean by that?' asked Khrest.

'Quite simple. My brother's rebel followers will attack and kidnap you the same way they did Rhodan. Unfortunately, I was unable to prevent this ambush, as you refused the escort I offered for your protection. Whatever happens between here and the spaceport is none of my concern. I hope you understand me. Ah, here they come!'

The door flew open and six soldiers rushed into the room. Their guns were pointed at the three men. Marshall could read hatred and determination in their thoughts.

Alban pointed at Khrest, Rathon and the telepath.

'Arrest them and take them down below. Lock them up together with Rhodan. The company will make him feel less lonely.'

Thus it happened that Rhodan had visitors barely ten minutes later. To his great surprise he saw how the three men were pushed into his cell, urged on by the gun butts of the dark-skinned Tuglanians. The door closed behind them.

Rhodan stood up and looked at Khrest, worry in his eyes.

'What's the meaning of this, Khrest? You don't mean to say that you were captured by the rebels?'

'The rebels? You could call them that. I'm sorry we had to accept this risk, but now, at least, we know which way the wind blows.'

'And they brought you here?'

'Brought us here? We're in Alban's palace.'

Rhodan did not hide his surprise. Then he pointed at the primitive seating arrangements with a gesture of invitation. 'Have a seat, gentlemen. I assume you'll have quite a few things to tell me. Begin, please!'

SEVEN

THE FLOATING BOMB

Wuriu Sengu winced imperceptibly. He glanced furtively in the direction of the next guard and then whispered to Reginald Bell.

'I've located them – Rhodan, Khrest, John Marshall and the Arkonide high commissioner of Tuglan. They're all sitting in a dark basement vault. Next to it is another prison. A youngish Tuglanian's lying on a bed. Judging by his clothing he must be a rather influential personality. Maybe Daros?'

Bell had listened intently. His thoughts were racing ahead. Rhodan and Khrest imprisoned? Here in the palace? Then Alban was a cheat after all! And if he and Sengu waited around here any longer they too would sooner or later land in jail.

This would not help matters at all. For nobody back on the *Stardust* had the faintest idea of Alban's treachery. Bell saw no possibility, either, of getting in touch with any of the mutants, for nothing of the sort had been prearranged. Therefore, Bell concluded: get out of here as fast as possible and return to the spacesphere!

'Come along, Sengu!' Bell began. He stood up. 'We have to leave here. I have only a small pocket ray gun on me that won't be of much help in case of need.'

The Japanese, too, rose from the bench where the two men had been sitting while awaiting a reply from Alban.

Hardly had the two men walked over to the nearest exit – not too fast to avoid looking suspicious – when a soldier coming from the opposite side ran after them. Behind him more men in uniform could be seen.

'The high Lord Alban is ready to receive you now,' reported the soldier zealously. Bell kept marching toward the door, unperturbed, and replied:

'Inform your Lord Alban to pay us a visit sometime at our spaceship – if he should feel so inclined. Our time has run out.'

The soldier hesitated. In the meantime the others had come closer. Two additional soldiers stood at the exit door, their weapons pointing halfway to the floor.

Bell was not willing to let himself be taken without resistance.

'Grab his gun!' he ordered Sengu, and from inside his pocket he began to shoot his own small ray gun. The two guards at the door felt the tingling of the energy pulses race through their bodies. Their limbs grew rigid; cramps shot through their hands and feet. They dropped their rifles. Seconds later they were rolling and tossing on the marble floor, screaming at the top of their lungs, trying in vain to lash out desperately at the invisible enemy. It did not occur to anybody to see the cause of their discomfort in Bell, who was still striding forward, his hands hidden in his pockets.

Sengu, meanwhile, had relieved the reluctant soldier of his weapon. One swift and expert Judo hold did the trick. He pointed the rifle at the other five guards, who were taken by surprise and could not reach fast enough for their ray guns.

'Just leave those guns where they are – don't reach!' warned Bell evenly. 'Just march ahead of us, straight to the main exit gate of the palace. And behave as naturally, as if nothing had happened, or else!'

'Lord Alban wishes to see you,' trembled one of the guards. 'He wants to talk to you.'

'Have him carry on a conversation with himself, then he's sure to be in the company of his equals. Let's go! By the way, how did the gyrocars with the policemen get up on that roof over there?'

They had meanwhile reached the palace courtyard and marched past the bewildered soldiers doing sentry duty, who stared after them with gaping mouths. No one dared a wrong move.

'They flew up there and then landed on the roof, sir. People were saying a little animal accomplished that with the help of some magic. Nobody can understand how it could be done.'

Bell grinned. That rascal Emby! What fun the mouse-beaver must have had, creating all that confusion among the Tuglanians. As long as he managed to achieve something of positive value with his perpetual playfulness! Where was the little fellow hiding now?

Sengu requisitioned a car and brought it over, along with its driver. Bell disarmed each of Alban's soldiers and then sent them back into the palace. Curious passers-by watched the whole incident from a respectful distance. They remained surprisingly passive. Apparently they did not care what happened to Alban and his soldiers.

Ten minutes later, Bell was back at the *Stardust* again and sounded the alarm.

It took quite a while until Karolan recovered from his surprise. Xaron related, meanwhile, the strange events he and his three men had witnessed. He described with loving detail the aerial acrobatics of the police cars, without trying to understand the incomprehensible.

The leader of the rebels bent down and gently petted Emby's silky fur on the back.

The mouse-beaver straightened up a bit, cocked his head and requested: 'Do it under my chin, please! That's where I like it best.'

Karolan almost toppled off his chair. 'He can talk, too?'

'Why, of course,' countered Xaron. 'He can talk. Didn't I mention it before? He belongs to the Arkonides.'

Karolan shook his head in amazement. 'Astonishing, really astonishing.' He kept stroking and gently scratching Emby's neck at the spot the Vagabondian preferred. Karolan's thoughts were tumbling all about. 'Perhaps he could help us to overthrow Alban. Maybe he can find Daros. Listen, little fellow, will you help in our fight to make Tuglan once more a loyal planet in the Arkonide empire?'

The mouse-beaver searched Karolan's thoughts and determined that he was speaking the truth. But before he could answer him, a man stormed into the room. Excited and out of breath he shouted:

'Rebellion! The inhabitants of Tugla are storming the palace! They say the Arkonides who landed here recently would help them to overthrow Alban, the traitor. Mysterious forces are already at work to punish the police for their misdeeds. Strange things have happened which can only be attributed to the Arkonides. People say this is a sign. They've decided to make Daros the next Lord of Tuglan.'

'That will suit us fine,' said Karolan. 'All the time we were forced to work secretly for that goal. Now we can came out in the open. Xaron, inform our men to take up arms and join the fight. We must help the rebellious citizens of Tugla. I'll come with you.' He looked at the little mouse-beaver. 'Do you want to join us?'

'Will I be able to play again?' asked Emby.

Karolan stared at him, stupefied. 'To play?'

'Of course, to play! What else? I've had such fun playing all day long today!'

Gradually it dawned on Karolan what Emby was trying to tell him.

'Ah – that's what you call playing? Why sure, you can play as much as you like. But let me make sure that you'll play with the right things and people. Do you promise!'

Emby's face became completely serious. 'Yes, I do promise. Is Rhodan also in the palace?'

'Rhodan?'

'Yes, the commander of our spaceship.'

Karolan exchanged meaningful glances with Xaron. 'For heaven's sake! Our little friend has put his paw on the right spot . . .'

Three minutes later, Karolan's men rushed out into the street and joined the excited citizens of Tugla in their march on the palace, where Alban's soldiers prepared themselves to defend Alban's life as well as their own.

Bell held a final conference with Major Deringhouse, the commander of the space-fighters that were waiting inside the mighty interior of the spacesphere, ready for a sortie.

'Ten fighters should be enough to teach Alban a lesson,' he said. 'We're not out to destroy anything wantonly or to kill any Tuglanians. Most of them were completely unaware of the real intentions of their ruler. But they have to learn, on the other hand, that nobody can fool around with us.'

'I'm worried about Rhodan,' confessed Deringhouse. 'The moment Alban understands what we're planning to do, he'll use Rhodan as a hostage.'

Bell's face took on a somber expression.

'Oh, don't talk such nonsense, Major! Nothing will happen to Rhodan. He let himself be captured deliberately, to find out the really responsible ones, and he has. Alban let his mask fall. Now we know where we're at, and we can act accordingly. Ten fighters, please. I'll drive ahead to the palace with an armored truck. We'll meet there. Wait for my instructions. We'll stay in touch via radio.'

Deringhouse saluted, faced about and left.

Bell had the mutants come to the Command Center, where he selected some of them.

'Now it's up to us to render Alban harmless before he can cause a lot of trouble. I believe that Ralf Marten and Kitai Ishibashi will be the right people for this purpose. As soon as we're close enough, they'll take over Alban's conscious mind and suggest the right thoughts to him; he'll then do anything we ask of him. The rest we'll discuss during our trip to Tugla. Let's go, the car's waiting.'

While the space-fighters, one after another, took off from the *Stardust* and shot skyward with moderate speed, the heavily armored tank started to roll. The spiral-shaped barrel of its pulse-ray cannon pointed in the direction of their final destination like a gigantic threatening finger. Somewhere in its innards hummed the small Arkonide reactor which supplied an unlimited amount of energy.

Bell informed the driver of the exact course they had to steer, then called Deringhouse over the radio.

'What can you see from up there?' he wanted to know.

Deringhouse responded right away.

'We're cruising above the palace. Down below we observe unusual excitement. From all sides people are hurrying toward the palace. Some of these citizens are armed. I wonder if the Lord has called on them to come and help defend the palace against us?'

'Who knows?' growled Bell and digested the unexpected bit of news. 'It seems strange, though. Continue your observations and inform us in case of any special new event. We're hurrying as fast as we can.'

Traffic grew heavier and heavier. Bell was struck by the realization that the Tuglanians did not seem especially astonished at the unexpected appearance of the Arkonide battle tank. He had expected panic and fear but just the opposite happened. The Tuglanians waved and cheered at the sight of the vehicle.

Bell turned to Fellmer Lloyd, one of the mutants. Lloyd was a so-called 'spotter.' He was not a genuine telepath but was capable of receiving and analyzing the brainwave patterns of living beings in his vicinity. It was easy for him to perceive danger or joy and a large variety of emotions.

'Lloyd, try to find out what's the matter with these people. Why aren't they frightened when they see us? By all rights they should assume that this is the beginning of our punitive action in retaliation for the bombing of the radio station.'

The heavy-set American concentrated. The other mutants remained silent so as not to disturb him.

Bell waited anxiously, all the while trying to make a way through the jubilant crowds. After two or three minutes Lloyd relaxed and said with a smile:

'As far as I can make out, they see us as allies. Their

preponderant mood is one of hatred and fury, but not toward us. They're filled with rebellious emotions. All are thinking of Lord Alban, spitefully and maliciously. They want to storm the palace and they believe we've come to help them.'

Bell nodded his head very slowly.

'Open rebellion . . . I see. The Tuglanians want to restore order. Our coming inspired them with the necessary courage. We mustn't disappoint them. They seem, therefore, to have always known that it was Alban and not Daros who wanted to rid them of the Arkonide empire.'

Fighting had already broken out in the vicinity of the palace. Some of Alban's soldiers had left the safety of the buildings and tried to disperse the crowds. They proceeded in a ruthless manner, which in turn incited the attackers all the more. Victims had fallen on both sides. The citizens of Tugla were poorly armed and often attacked the soldiers with their bare hands.

From somewhere the howling of sirens could be heard. A column of cars appeared from around the corner and stopped abruptly. Armed civilians jumped out of the cars. Their first maneuvers showed plainly that they had been trained for street fighting. They brandished their weapons and called out to the soldiers and citizens:

'Long live Lord Daros! Long live the empire! Down with Alban, the traitor!'

'Long live Lord Daros!' The citizens picked up the cry and with renewed hope and confidence stormed toward the soldiers, whose courage began to flag. Karolan's rebel forces had entered into the battle.

Bell, meanwhile, had arrived at the palace gates. Deringhouse reported that he saw pulse-ray cannons mounted in the courtyard, ready to defend the palace to the last man. He requested orders for his fighter planes.

'Try to disrupt their plans and installations of defense,' suggested Bell. 'But remember, Rhodan and Khrest are being held prisoners inside the palace. I'll put Sengu to work to get our proper bearings.'

The Japanese 'saw' through the palace walls. Softly he reported:

'Khrest, Rhodan, Rathon and Marshall are still in their prison cell. Close nearby is the young Tuglanian we suppose to be Daros. The guards have been withdrawn. I'm searching for Alban now.'

The space-fighters went into a dive and sprayed the soldiers inside the courtyards with electron showers. Bell, in turn, placed the palace gates under bombardment. The huge gate nearest to his gigantic armored tank began to glow and then collapsed. Without paying attention to the dangerous heat, the impatient civilians stormed through the breach and thronged into the palace grounds.

Karolan decided to try his luck at another spot. Together with his troop he entered a side street and approached the palace from the rear. His car column followed slowly behind. They were shot at sporadically from the palace walls but they suffered no casualties.

And then, all of a sudden, there was Emby again!

The mouse-beaver had waited patiently in the car until Karolan gave the prearranged signal, whereupon Emby leaped from the car, waddling proudly through the lines of of the grinning rebels. The other civilians interrupted their enthusiastic cheering for a moment and stared in amazement at the funny little creature that walked upright like a man and showed no signs of fear. Some of the crowd had already heard of the strange events that had occurred in connection with this animal. The appearance of Emby made their hopes soar.

The pavement near Emby was hit by an energy ray and began to melt.

The mouse-beaver looked up and noticed several soldiers taking cover behind a parapet. Karolan nodded to Emby encouragingly, as if to say: 'Go ahead, play! Have fun!'

Amidst shouts of horror, and with outstretched arms, the soldiers involuntarily left their hiding place, sailing down like swallows with a gentle slant, and landed right in the middle of the crowd of waiting rebels, who received them in a none too friendly manner.

Karolan ordered the column to stop and pointed to a small gate in the wall.

'Here it is,' he murmured. 'Nobody will expect us to force our entry at this place. Xaron, the bomb!'

Xaron's face expressed doubt. 'Remember, Karolan, this bomb has a devastating effect. We can't take cover here. Couldn't Emby perhaps . . . ?'

Karolan understood at once. He called Emby over to him.

'You see this black ball here, Emby? If I push this button it will take exactly fifteen seconds till this ball will explode and destroy everything in its vicinity. Do you understand?'

Emby looked at him solemnly. 'I know what you want. You'd like that ball placed *on the other side* of the gate, to explode and cause the obstacle to be pushed outward. All right. Push the button and put the ball in front of you on the ground.'

Hastily Karolan obeyed Emby's instructions, then started to count: 'One – two – three –'

Emby fixed his eyes on the bomb. After all, if he was

capable of causing cars and armoured vehicles to parade high up in the air, this little object would present no difficulty. His mind began to radiate impulses and . . .

'Six – seven – eight –'

The bomb was lifted gently off the ground and floated up toward the top of the wall. Perplexed faces stared down from there at the miracle of the flying black sphere, not knowing what to do with it. The rebels waited breathlessly. Only Karolan, unperturbed, kept on counting. 'Nine – ten – eleven –'

Swaying to and fro, the bomb circled the head of a soldier. The soldier clumsily tried to seize it. Then the bomb disappeared from the view of Karolan and the rest of the onlookers outside the gate.

'Twelve – thirteen –'

Without any command, the crowd dissolved and pressed close to the wall. The space in front of the gate was clear of people. Nobody wanted to be hit by bomb fragments. The faces up on the wall disappeared.

'Fourteen –'

Emby felt someone seize him by the paw and jerk him to the side. This caused him to lose control over the pretty ball. And so he simply let go of it. As chance would have it, the bomb dropped to the ground exactly in back of the gate.

'Fifteen!' said Karolan and threw himself to the ground, pulling Emby after him.

A blinding flash obliterated the blue sun in the sky for several seconds. An ear-splitting explosion roared through the street, reverberating from the walls of the houses. A wide gap yawned where the gate had been.

'Long Live Lord Daros!' yelled Karolan and jumped to his feet. 'Down with Alban, the traitor!'

The rebels and the civilians swarmed into the palace. Emby leaped to safety, jumping aside and out of the way of the trampling hordes. He waited until the crowd in the street had thinned out, then followed them slowly into the courtyard. Somewhere inside this palace Rhodan was sure to be, as well as his friend Bell. But first of all he wanted to show Alban some of his fine tricks. That tyrant would take a trip through the air, like nobody else before!

And while desperate battles were fought inside the courtyard, Emby crawled through a narrow basement window into the subterranean vaults of the palace in order to search for Alban and Rhodan.

EIGHT

THE DEATH OF ...

Lord Alban realized that his game was up. He had but one ace up his sleeve: the captured Arkonides.

His pulse-ray cannons had been put out of commission by the swift space-fighters. An armored tank had penetrated the palace courtyard. His soldiers surrendered to the enemy wherever they could. The rebels and his brother's friends were already storming through the halls of his palace.

Alban seized his heavy pulse-ray pistol and left the room from which he had directed the battle and had woven his intrigues. Determined to fight to the bitter end, he hurried down to the underground vaults to prepare for the final act of the drama. But first he switched on the loudspeakers of the palace intercom to make sure that the message he had spoken on tape a few minutes earlier would be loudly carried to every corner of the palace.

Bell heard the voice of the traitor as he got out of the battle tank to lead his mutants into the palace.

'If the Arkonides desire to see their leader alive, they must cease fighting immediately. I'm now with Khrest and Rhodan. I shall kill them unless the rebels and the Arkonides have cleared out of the palace grounds within five minutes. This is my one and only offer. I repeat: If the Arkonides ...'

'Damn it!' Bell cursed and glanced helplessly in the direction of Lloyd and Sengu. 'Where's Rhodan? Can't you locate him, Sengu?'

'I can see him, down in this direction,' said the Japanese. 'Alban's just about to enter the cell. He's armed. Now he's pointing his weapon at Rhodan. I can't properly judge the distance from here.'

'Let's go!' Bell commanded. Quickly he removed the red contact lenses from his eyes. 'We'll show him who he's dealing with! Sengu, correct the direction if we're going the wrong way. But hurry!'

And still – Bell almost didn't make it in time, if it had not been for . . .

Rhodan listened intently for the slightest noise that filtered through to their prison cell. There was fighting going on outside. The hissing of the pulse-ray shots mingled with desperate cries. In between came the powerful blast of an explosion. Pretty close! Then silence, soon followed by screaming and shouting! Hurried footsteps, running far above in the corridors and halls of the palace. The shots fell less frequently now. Only once could he distinguish the typical buzzing sound of an Arkonide pulse-ray gun. That must be Bell with his mutants.

And then came the distorted voice of Lord Alban over one of the loudspeakers, relaying his last message.

Rhodan drew himself up to his full height.

'Alban's made his decision. He's going to kill us if he can't use us as hostages. Khrest, lie down on the bed and remain completely still, please. I'll talk with Alban. Marshall, you stand behind the door and try to overpower Alban when he enters the cell. Rathon, you too, do nothing. Is that clear?'

Khrest shook his head. 'It's useless, we have no weapons. How can you defend yourself against a ray gun?'

'Wait and see, Khrest. Those who give up the fight so easily don't deserve to rule an empire.'

The Arkonide scientist gazed long into Rhodan's eyes, then slowly he nodded his head; he had understood. Without a word he stretched out on the bed. Beads of perspiration covered his forehead.

Marshall, who had freed Rhodan from his handcuffs, was quicker to comprehend the situation. He stepped behind the door and waited, a resolute expression on his face.

Steps were coming closer.

Actually, thought Rhodan, *this is the first time in my entire life that I'm facing imminent death. I cannot defend myself. I'm at the mercy of a desperate man who can neither gain nor lose from my death. My chances are very slim, much smaller than my friends could guess. Actually, we have no chances whatsoever! It was shortsighted of me to get us all voluntarily into this situation.*

The steps came to a halt in front of the cell door.

A key turned in the lock.

Our time has come, thought Rhodan with calm determination. *Whether we come through now or fail will depend on whether we react fast enough, if we can bluff Alban. If only we can string him along long enough for Bell to find us! Bell's our last hope now!*

The door opened slightly. A swift kick made it fly open all the way. The first thing Rhodan saw was the spiral-shaped barrel of a dangerous looking weapon – pointed directly at him! Behind it he could make out Alban, standing in the dimly lit corridor, keeping at a distance from the door. His thumb rested on the firing button.

'I can see only three Arkonides,' he said, strangely calm. 'Where's the fourth man? Is he behind the door? Unless he steps forward I'll shoot at once.'

Rhodan saw the icy-cold eyes of Alban and knew he meant what he said. Marshall, the telepath, realized the danger even faster. With a resigned shrug of his shoulders he left his hiding place to stand next to Rhodan.

Alban, with obvious satisfaction, nodded and kept the four prisoners covered with his ray pistol.

'I suppose you've heard my proclamation – it's your life against mine. You've no other choice left.'

'You're defying the empire,' warned Rhodan in order to win time. Bell must be inside the palace by now. Perhaps one of the mutants would still manage to seize control of Alban's brain in time.

'One of you will go upstairs now and relay your order to withdraw from the palace. Then you'll accompany me to a secret hanger below the roof where I have a small rocketship waiting. As soon as I've started you'll be free.'

'He's bluffing,' warned Marshall. 'He plans to shoot us before his escape.'

'I thought so,' said Rhodan. 'Well, how about it, Alban?'

For a moment the Lord was dumbfounded, then his face contorted with fury.

From somewhere out in the corridor came a sound as if something were being softly dragged along the ground. In between, the gentle padding of soft paws. John Marshall said in English:

'Somebody's approaching. I can sense his thoughts. Peculiar thought streams. My God – it's Emby! He's looking for us.'

We must keep stalling, thought Rhodan desperately. *Just a bit longer. Maybe Emby can help us. But how does he know about our dangerous situation?*

'Answer!' shouted Alban, nervously fingering the trigger of his weapon. In his present state of mind the Tuglanian was extremely dangerous, his reactions those of an insane man. No knowing what he would do the next moment. 'Answer or all will be over!'

Rhodan felt the feverish excitement that gripped every one in the room. He strained his ears but could no longer hear the noise that had come from the corridor outside. Shouts rang out, far away, hollow and muffled. A door slammed; it sounded like a shot.

'Who's to accompany you?' Rhodan asked.

Alban seemed relieved, but then his mistrust won out. Once more his fingers tightened around the ray pistol.

'You want to trick me, Arkonide. It's probably better if I kill you all right now. I'll . . .'

Then the thing happened that Rhodan had so fervently hoped for.

Lord Alban felt a mighty blow from an invisible fist strike his back. His pistol came to life and rose with a will of its own toward the ceiling, barely fifteen feet above the floor of the corridor.

Alban could not understand how his pistol could suddenly defy gravity but under no circumstances did he wish to let go of it now. He clung to it with all his might and, naturally, was inexorably pulled up along with it. His legs kicked desperately in the air as he lost the firm ground beneath his feet. He was suspended from the barrel of his gun as though from a horizontal bar that was being pulled upward by invisible ropes.

Then the gun touched the rough ceiling, wedging

the fingers of the hapless Alban tightly in between. Howling with pain, Alban let go and dashed to the ground.

He did not fall a great distance, true. But, unfortunately for him, he twisted his body during his fall and as his feet slammed forcibly into the floor, his body jackknifed and his head bounced sideways, hitting a sharp protruding pillar of the wall.

There was a dull thud. Alban collapsed. His body grew limp.

Rhodan saw at once that Alban was beyond all help. He was dead.

A noise from behind startled Rhodan. He turned around quickly and looked straight into Emby's brown eyes, peering up at him like those of a faithful, trusting and very pleased dog.

'Down with Alban, the traitor!' he squeaked merrily and then his voice changed to a bright chirping tone. 'Long live the galactic empire and the new Lord Daros!'

Khrest, Rathon and Marshall had stepped out into the corridor, too. Gradually, the tremendous tension of the last few minutes was subsiding. Khrest smiled weakly.

'That was a close call – a last minute reprieve.'

'Much too close for comfort,' remarked Rhodan. 'But we can leave Tuglan now knowing for sure we've installed the right Lord as ruler. But, first, we have to find him!'

Steps came closer, became louder and more forceful. Then a well-known voice roared:

'It must be here somewhere – that door over there! What are you saying, Sengu? *What?* That beast of a mouse? With Rhodan? Impossible! I'll die if that thing beat us to it! Sticking his nose into everything!'

Light flooded the corridor. Bell stormed down the

hall, stopping abruptly the moment he noticed the group around his friend Rhodan. He shook his fist at Emby, who sat at Rhodan's feet. The little fellow concentrated blissfuly on having his chin tickled and gently stroked.

'You damned Mickey Mouse, you! Won't you leave anything for me to do? If I get my hands on you you'll end up in the nearest cooking pot!'

Bell's threats changed rapidly to furious protests as he floated toward the ceiling. Soon his back touched the stony vault and Emby twittered joyfully:

'I'll keep you there till you die of hunger, if you don't behave nice. Well, are you going to behave?'

Bell grunted a reply nobody could understand. The mutants, who had joined the group meanwhile, laughed at the ludicrous sight. Even Rhodan could not help grinning.

In the midst of it all, the Japanese Sengu said suddenly:

'We must set Daros free. He's in the next cell. And more people are imprisoned down here.'

Nobody paid the least attention now to Bell who, helplessly, was struggling with his hands and feet to climb *down* the walls.

Energy rays melted the lock of the cell door. Seconds later a very frightened Daros was brought out of the dark vault.

The next day the *Stardust* left the planet Tuglan. From the high commissioner's robots Rhodan had obtained the exact data he needed for the hyperjump to the Vega system. He had ordered the robots to keep strict silence about the entire Tuglanian interlude. He knew he could rely on them to obey his instructions as his rank in the

Arkonide hierarchy was even higher than Rathon's.

Daros had been appointed the new Lord by the inhabitants of Tuglan and the united planets of the Laton system. He signed a trade treaty with Khrest, acting as the official Arkonide representative, which would become effective at a later date at the right opportunity.

Rathon was promised that he would shortly receive a new hyperwave installation to reestablish contact with the empire. Rhodan did not commit himself as to the exact date.

While the planet Tuglan sank away into the depths of the universe, and while the *Stardust* was surging forward to the point of transition, Rhodan took special care to insure the presence of not only Khrest, Thora and Bell in the Command Center, but particularly that of Emby – the playbeaver!'

A short while before the transition Bell spoke up after he had visibly been laboring under some thoughts.

'When you stop to consider it, we made a quite unnecessary detour to Tuglan. Tuglan had really nothing to do with our search for the planet of eternal life – or was the problem on Tuglan another part of the Galactic Riddle?'

'If so, then only in a roundabout way,' replied Rhodan. 'But you're wrong if you believe that our Tuglanian adventure was of no value to us. Without our intervention Alban would've put his evil plans into effect. Tuglan would've been lost to the empire.'

'And since Emby with his playfulness brought about our temporary stay on Tuglan, the Arkonide empire will give him the credit for our successful mission there?' Bell did not sound too happy.

Rhodan appeared unusually serious as he replied:

'That's quite possible. I must admit that Emby managed to squeeze us into a tight corner, but nobody can deny that he didn't do his very best to get us out of it again! Without his help I'd probably be dead by now.'

Rhodan bent down to the mouse-beaver and gently stroked his fur. Emby was purring not unlike a cat.

Thora joined the little group. 'Once we reach the Vega system we'll be able to calculate the position of the planet of the immortals. There's no point in delaying any futher – we must resume our search at once! My patience is thoroughly exhausted!'

'You're being unfair, Thora.' The voice that spoke was cool and passionless and to everyone's surprise it was her fellow Arkonide who took up the defence of Rhodan. Khrest continued: 'We returned law and order to Tuglan. We witnessed with our own eyes how efficiently this was accomplished by our Terran friends. They're powerful allies in an attempt to revitalize our decaying star realm. I fully trust Rhodan in his promise that one day he'll bring us back to Arkon. But I realize this longed for homecoming can only come about when the time's propitious – and the right moment hasn't come yet.'

He made a slight bow in Thora's direction, then absented himself silently from the Command Center and returned to his cabin. The beauteous Arkonide was obviously startled by Khrest's admonition but without protest followed the great scientist from the room, politely nodding good-bye to Rhodan and Bell.

A green light glowed, indicating imminent transition. Rhodan stooped down to Emby.

'No nonsense now, young fellow! We're friends now, aren't we? And you know I'm the commander of this ship, don't you? Then you also know you have to obey me – no playing around now!'

Perry placed a hand on the transition lever.

'Commander Rhodan, I promise to obey you!' the little mouse-beaver chirped solemnly, scant seconds before the hyperjump that would transport them over a distance of thirty-five thousand light-years to the Vega system. 'But I'll never obey that red-haired monster at your side –'

Bell bristled but the tension was broken when a new voice spoke up, a young voice with an infectious laugh. Voice and laugh belonged to a young crewman from Independence, Missouri, back home on Earth. His hobby was xenophilology. It served him well now.

Spaceman First Class Phillip Callen spoke words which, in a matter of moments, would lead him to speak a name destined to become famous throughout far expanses of the space-time continuum. Spontaneously, he would christen the impish alien from Vagabond who heretofore had answered only to Emby, M.B., the initials for what he was: a mouse-beaver.

'Shades of Shakespeare,' Phillip Callen began, 'If Emby doesn't have the personality of Puck!'

'Puck?' echoed Bell.

The young spaceman suddenly wondered if his thoughts were welcome to the commander and his friends but Perry set his mind at ease by smiling and saying, 'I think I know what you mean.'

Phillip, encouraged, continued: 'Puck – from *Midsummer Night's Dream.* Originally thought, by the people of the sixteenth century, to be a mischievous spirit, a tricky sprite.'

'More of a *Midsummer Night's* Nightmare! I'd call him,' growled Bell.

All laughed.

'Well, the little skeezer's certainly plucky!' said Phillip. 'Plucky Puck! Say –'

'Yes?' Did Rhodan antipate the boy's next thought but graciously refrain from speaking? The world would never know, but his nature was very kind, and it was very likely so. In any event, it was Phillip Callen, Spaceman First Class, aboard the stellar sphere *Stardust II*, bound for Vega, who spoke and said:

'Pucky!'

'Pucky!' As one, all repeated the name. Even the mouse-beaver squeaked it, bidding good-bye forever to Emby, accepting himself forever after as . . . Pucky.

And, with the leader of the New Power, the Peacelord of the Universe, the normal men and mutants, Pucky was on his way to the ultimate confrontation with the Immortal.